Look at Me

Look at Me

Robert Shoub

QUATTRO BOOKS

The publication of *Look at Me* has been generously supported by the Canada Council for the Arts and the Ontario Arts Council.

Canada Council for the Arts Conseil des Arts du Canada

ONTARIO ARTS COUNCIL CONSEIL DES ARTS DE L'ONTARIO
50 YEARS OF ONTARIO GOVERNMENT SUPPORT OF THE ARTS
50 ANS DE SOUTIEN DU GOUVERNEMENT DE L'ONTARIO AUX ARTS

Author photo: Deborah Hiscock
Cover design: Sarah Beaudin
Cover image: Christian Hebell
Editor: Luciano Iacobelli
Typography: Grey Wolf Typography

Library and Archives Canada Cataloguing in Publication

Shoub, Robert, author
Look at me / Robert Shoub.

ISBN 978-1-927443-61-3 (pbk.)
I. Title.
PS8637.H675L65 2014 C813'.6 C2014-902307-3

Published by Quattro Books Inc.
Toronto

info@quattrobooks.ca
www.quattrobooks.ca

Printed in Canada

I love the sound of breaking glass
Especially when I'm lonely.
I need the noises of destruction
When there's nothing new.

– Nick Lowe

Here it is. The real deal. I know I don't have much time. I know the cops will be here any minute. I just wanted to tell everybody how it happened, and I figured this video would be the best way. I don't really know *why* it happened. I'm not making excuses. Fuck that. I just know there's going to be a lot of heat and noise, and I'm thinking this is my shot at putting out the truth, whatever that means. Plus, it should be good for the movie version.

How do I look? I know the mask is a little creepy, but it's for the dramatic reveal at the end … you know who I am already, but it'll just make for a bigger moment – it's like my own little movie. Plus, they may use it for the end credits. Anyways, for now, just sit back and enjoy the ride. You know what I look like. I think you'd agree that I look pretty good, like in a Taylor Lautner kind of way. Not that I'm vain or anything, but, appearances matter, right? Everybody judges, right? I'm no different.

So here it goes. By the time you see this, it will all be over. Well, that's not really true. I figure there will be lots of interviews, probably some spots for my parents on the talk shows, maybe a book deal for me, before the film deal. I'm hoping for a feature, but if that doesn't work, at least an HBO doc.

You probably think I'm a freak, or a psycho or whatever. I really am sorry I did this. Really. Is it *all* my fault? No way. The weird thing is, I don't really know how I feel about it all. I mean, I have feelings, for sure, but … it's complicated.

Why did I do it? That's what everybody will ask. Like, how could someone be so fucked up, right? You know, I really wish I could just tell you straight and simple. Really. You'll probably think I'm some kind of monster, right? And somehow saying "I'm sorry" just doesn't really cut it, right? "I'm sorry" is for normal, regular screw-ups. I'm sorry I stole your iPhone. I'm sorry I called you a fag. I'm sorry I fucked your girlfriend. *This* shit? This one gets a two-week media saturation cycle. This one gets you your own Wikipedia entry. Look, I guess I really do feel bad about it. Believe it or not, I never wanted to hurt anybody. I just can't understand why it happened, and maybe that's what this video is all about now. Maybe if I can get my head around what happened, *then* maybe I can feel something more about it, and figure out the why. They'll call me a psycho, I know. But I'm not. I know what I did was wrong. I get it. And I do feel bad. It's just … so big. But I wanted big. That was the whole idea. Go big or go home. But I fucked up. But you know, there's part of me now that just feels … relieved. And relief is good, right? So I guess part of me feels kind of good about it. Like I said … pretty fucking complicated. It all happened so quickly, and even when I thought I was in total control, I guess I wasn't. I don't really want to think about it at all, but if I don't think about it, then you'll think I'm a psycho. So I lose either way, and I guess I deserve that.

They say ya gotta believe! Me, I don't believe in anything. Well, I used to believe in myself. That's one thing my teachers always talk about. *Believe in yourself. You can make a difference.* They're right. I know I have! It's pretty clear to me that I can't believe in anything else. I mean, like, what else could I believe in? My government? My church? The *system*? Money? I used to believe in all that stuff. Not anymore. They're all lies. Everything, everyone, promises you something, but they're all illusions in the end. We should all be really honest and just say it's all about *making it,* getting a first-class ticket, and doing it up big! But you didn't click here for a lecture, you're here for *The Inside, Up-Close Look at Adolescent Alienation – The Breakdown into Psychosis of Today's Teenagers!*

Right after these messages!

Fuck – where to begin? My name is .... Nah, boring and pointless. You know my name. What will the talking heads tell you? That I was an underachieving, alienated, bullied, sexually frustrated middle-class teenager who went for attention in the only way left for him? Bullshit. That my parents failed me? Bullshit. That my teachers failed me? My church failed me? My friends failed me? Bullshit bullshit bullshit. I was pulling down an "A" average, with several great university offers. Engineering, with a minor in Chemistry, or maybe an MBA. Working on a few scholarships too. And check this out – can you see this? Hope the camera can make this out ... it's a Divisional Championship Football trophy from two years ago. This other one was for second place in a Debating Championship. You impressed? I was, for a while. But all that got boring. So whatever. But hey, let's get the background out of the way, right? My parents, well, they've been shittily married more than twenty years. I've got an older brother, younger sister. My brother Harper – he's an Actualizations and Paradigms Enabler for CPU – Creative Potentials Unlimited. He's only twenty-five and he's pulling in six figures, just like my dad. Working in California. Then there's my sister Krystal. She's a part-time cheerleader and full-time bitch.

She's working on her goal of a career in nuclear medicine, maybe law, then going into politics, and having an awesome singing and acting career in her spare time. Very big in the brain, but very cold around the heart. Kind of lives up to her name – great to look at and hard as nails. Had a dog – Kahlua – stupid fucking name for a dog – not my idea. The shrinks will probably say that I was incapable of feeling emotion, or empathy or something, but that's bullshit, because I loved that dog, right up to when he died, which was *not* my fault. A little chemistry experiment, sure, but it wasn't meant for him! Stupid animals, dogs. Anyway, we're just a great, happy family, maybe a little messed up, but, you know, who isn't, really? Our family is like a white version of *The Cosby Show*. Actually, the Huxtables weren't so black if you ask me. I love that bit when Theo comes home with a bad report card, and he's telling Cosby that he should love him unconditionally, no matter what, because he's his son and he should accept his weaknesses and all that shit, and everybody in the audience is going "*aaawwww* ..." like all sentimental, and Cosby comes back with, "*Boy, I brought you into this world, and I can take you out.*" Everybody laughs. Cosby the killer. That's right.

Fuck. I'm sorry about all those kids, OK?

So, *my happy family*. My mom – her name's Lauren – works as an upscale real estate agent – only handles properties over a mil. Lots of those. She also flips a lot of properties herself – buys them, gets her crew to work them over for a month or two, then resells them for more. Way more. I've gone with her to a few open houses, just to check out some killer cribs. Actually, she likes it when I go with her, because she sometimes gets spooked – she tells me that there's a lot of violent crime in showing upscale houses – she's heard of some real estate agents being held up, or even raped. She carries mace and a small caliber gun – I think a .32. Anyways, I've seen some really cool places. There was one with an indoor lap pool – you just swim and stay in one place with this current flowing past you, *and* an outdoor infinity pool, where the water goes right to the edge at one end, so you're lying in it and just staring off like it's the ocean, never ending. Plus it had a fully equipped digital front projection theatre with a twenty-foot screen, popcorn machine, the whole place wired for sound with hidden speakers, sauna wired for audio, heated garage, wine cellar – man, why would anybody sell that? I'd never leave a place like that. Goodbye world, see you later. What else do you need?

It was kind of spooky walking around other people's homes. I'd always take a little something, just a tiny piece from the place. I don't know why. Maybe just because I could. It just felt kind of cool. So, anyways, now I have this drawer filled with ashtrays and cutlery and fridge magnets and shells and pens and even a few photos. Sometimes I make up little stories in my mind about all these people. What their lives were like.

I went with my mom to one house that was done in this real clean way, all granite and glass, everything grey and shiny. Metal and stone. Very classy. Very cool. Kind of like our place. In one room they actually had a tree, like a huge tree trunk going from the floor to the ceiling, with branches and everything – no leaves though. Get this – it was coated in plastic sealant. My mom told me that they'd injected the tree with a plastic chemical to totally seal it up. It had little photos in plastic sleeves hanging from the branches – I took one. I called this thing the Tree of Wishes and made up a story about how the tree had magic in it, how in ancient times people would come to make wishes for their future and leave things in a hole in the trunk. The people who lived in this house had heard about this. When they bought the property they decided to put the tree inside their house, and preserve it forever, and the photos were their way of making their wishes. But the gods were angry at them for cutting the tree down, so the whole family died in a fiery car accident … or something like that. Anyway, writing stories hasn't helped me out too much, as you'll soon see. I wish I could re-write my life story, but I guess I wasn't really the only author of that one. I wonder who'll write the movie version?

I was thinking about making a book of these stories. I could be a pretty good writer. I'm really good at it – at least that's what my teachers say. I don't see how it's a big deal. Like I said, I do well in all my classes. I just don't feel the work is that hard, and there's lots of ways to get it done. Red Bull, maybe some of my mom's diet uppers, maybe a little coke for the energy, then some grass to mellow me out when I'm done – I can stay up for two days, sometimes three. You can get a lot of work done without any sleep. Of course, then you have to crash, but twenty-four hours of sleep on a weekend or a slow day of school usually takes care of that. I just surf for paper mills, buy a couple for each assignment, maybe mix and match, maybe not. Some classes, the math and science ones, you have to know your stuff, because you know, they'll test you in those. Not so hard, just formulas really. I guess I got a good brain for that. Very methodical. Anyways, they say I can write. There's a formula for that too. It's just like pushing around metaphors, some personification, maybe slap some sentimental crap in there, how awful I feel, how beautiful nature is, how crazy the world is. *The autumn morning whispers / The flowers sing their mourning songs / My heart moans in its red cage.* They go nuts for it. Actually, I guess I kind of like doing it. I've written some cool raps, and a few short stories. Also some fan fiction stuff. I wrote a couple of stories about the stuff I've taken from these houses. It comes to me pretty easily. My imagination just gets going and the stories flow through my head. I really don't find schoolwork so hard, but it is boring. It's really not hard to do well, but it is hard to care. I mean, it's almost impossible to see the connection between what I'm doing and the real world most of the time. The world is burning up in front of us, and they've got me conjugating verbs and memorizing who fought in some battle a century ago. Yawn.

I don't see much of my dad, and that used to bug me, but I'm used to it now. He's a Director of Experiential Marketing for IC – International Concepts and Integrated Communications. He's got a great name – Luke – it's got this kind of cool cowboy vibe to it, and everybody always throws *Star Wars* lines at him, which he loves. You could call him Skywalker for all the travelling he does. I mean, seriously, I never see him. It probably doesn't matter much because he's not the best communicator. Which is kind of ironic when you think about where he works. But maybe there's some other kind of communication that I don't know about. Anyway, he tells me that I can be the best at whatever I want to do. He tells me that life is for winners, and that's what it's all about. He says it's not about trying – nobody *really* respects someone who tries and loses. He says history is written by the winners, and that's who we respect. That about sums up everything my dad's ever said to me. We don't *talk* a lot – like I said, he's not around, and when he is, there doesn't seem to be much to say. But it's OK. Whenever he comes back, he always brings me a guilt gift. I've got lots of cool gear.

I've played all the best videogames, so I'm a kind of an expert. Right now I'd say that *Half Life 2* is probably the best first-person game out there. My favourites would be hard to say, although I've loved *Carmageddon* with all the *Death Race 2000* kills, especially the old lady, and what really rocks is wiping the blood off the windshield. *Gears of War* also has good blood on screen, and using corpses as human shields is sweet. Good kill with the chainsaw up the groin. *Thrill Kill* was never officially released, but you can get a bootleg copy. Nice kills with lots of different stuff – syringes and cattle prods to severed limbs. You need three other players though. *God of War* is pretty cool when you shift to the perspective of the creature you are killing. Ripping the eyes out of the Cyclops is pretty cool. Lots of decapitations and limb removals. I learned a lot about the Greek gods and Greek mythology from that one. *Condemned 2: Bloodshot* is very cool, sort of like a *CSI* gone psycho trip … you don't know if it's the special agent's own personal demons or some other psycho he's whacking, but the first-person perspective is great in the alleys, plus you get to do a little crime scene analysis when you're not wailing on a guy with a baseball bat. *Manhunt* really holds up, very creepy, especially with the whole snuff-film vibe. Superviolence, with lots of impaling and intense suffering from the victim. You can suffocate a guy with a plastic bag and cut his jugular and he really squirms and cries as he bleeds out. I heard they took out a castration scene before its release. I suppose everybody's played the *Mortal Kombat* series, and they've gotten better and better. But I think that series has been outdone by *Grand Theft Auto*. You can do so much with those. Having sex with prostitutes and then frying them with a flamethrower is so wild. Plus you get your money back! Great 3D, especially with the car chases and gang fights. *Postal 2* is pretty wild too, especially using cats jammed over your gun for a silencer, or hitting people with anthrax-filled cow heads! Hilarious! Like, who gets paid to come up with this stuff? I'd do it for free! I actually think

I'd be a great game designer. I love action movies, and I watch tons of old movies and TV shows all the time, mostly to check out the action choreography and framing. I could set up the best action sequences in the world. A few of my buddies were into this too, sort of like a club, with me as its president. It's way cool watching the old action movies, digging them up. I mean, everybody can watch the new ones, and I'm always going on about them – movies, TV shows, videogames, it's not that big of a deal I guess. It's just what everybody is into, right? Only I probably know a lot more. Not to brag, that's just how it is.

We had a debate in our English class about videogame violence and its effect on us. Now, I'm pretty good at debating. I argued against it. There's no proof, and really, no reasonable argument for censoring these, really. I mean, why stop with the games? You know, everybody says they desensitize us, but you know what? I'm not retarded – oh, *sorry* ... I mean "mentally differentiated." Obviously I know they're not real. In fact, I argued that it was like a good release for us to let our frustrations and anger out in a peaceful way! My English teacher Mr. Adams called this "catharsis," which was a word the Greeks invented. So please, don't tell me that it was media violence that made me do it. Shit, if it wasn't for videogames, I probably would have got into even *more* trouble than I'm in now. Although I guess that's pretty hard to imagine.

Like I said before, I never wanted to hurt anyone. I know you probably won't believe me, but you could try. It really wasn't my fault. It was as much Jeremy's fault as mine. More on him in a sec. You're probably wondering why I would want to do it anyway, right? I can't give you a solid answer on that, but stick around and maybe *you* can figure it, out – then you can let *me* know.

So, a bit more about my family, maybe that will help. Like I was saying, my dad isn't around much. I actually think I've seen him more on Skype in the last few years than I have in person. My mom's a close second. The way they get along, I think it's a planned thing. Reminds me of *Up In The Air*, that George Clooney flick. Kind of boring – I only checked it out because I heard my mom and dad arguing about which of them it was more about. I'd call it a tie – my dad's the flier, but my mom's a cold-hearted shark, she'd be perfect for firing people like Clooney does in the movie. My mother missed my seventeenth birthday to go close on a house, but whatever. There's a scene in the movie where Clooney is hitting on this woman he just met in a hotel bar, and they're comparing all their credit cards. Getting all turned on – *"Hey is that carbon fiber?" "No, graphite."* Clooney is going for ten million frequent flyer miles. That's my old man. I've actually lifted cards from him – just to see if he would notice they were gone. No problems. I know they've both screwed around – they said they were working on staying together for Krystal and me, but that's bullshit. Nothing's changed. They're together for money. I figure with the pre-nup and the legal fees and tax breaks, it's just cheaper for them to stay cohabitating.

I can't remember the last time either one of them said they loved me. Maybe online. Not sure. Whatever. I used to be kind of angry with them, but I'm over that now. I mean, I can see why they are how they are. *Their* parents never speak to *them*, so, you know, that's how they roll with me. Luke's dad died a long time ago, and his mom lives in some gated golf-course in Mexico. We went to see her a few years ago, and all she did was talk about how shitty the servants were, or how great she was at golf. All she wanted to do was play cards and drink a lot of gin and tonics. Whatever. Lauren's mom and dad are both still around, but we haven't seen them for years either. We went for Thanksgiving once, and all I remember is everybody drinking a lot, and my granddad constantly trying to grab Lauren's ass. I thought it was pretty funny then, but now it just seems creepy. Luke got pissed off about it, and my grandma just sat there staring into her drink. I remember a bit of shouting, and dinner being so quiet that all you heard was cutlery tinkling on china, and then a silent ride home. Lauren never talks about them now.

In our film class, our teacher showed us this film, *Rope*. Kind of boring, but a cool idea. These two guys kill another guy, stow him in a big wooden chest in their apartment and then invite all his family and friends over for a party. It's supposed to be in *real time*, like 24. They do it just to see if they *can*. Like it's a test for themselves. They invite one of their college professors over, who taught them about Nietzsche and the *Ubermensch*, which is German for Superman. At first I couldn't really follow what he was talking about, but it had something to do with God being dead, and a new kind of man who advances himself to create his own values to be better than everybody else's. Or something like that. Sounds all right to me. Sometimes I think *I* wanted to do it just to see if I could. But get this – the comic book Superman was *originally* an evil villain, modeled after this Nietzsche idea. Wild, right? He was a regular guy, pulled out of a bread line by this crazy scientist, and given a drug that gave him telepathic powers. He used them for evil acts, like killing the scientist for starters. Check this out – he even looked like Lex Luthor, bald and snarly. It was only later that he got turned into a Super*Hero*, because the writer realized he could sell more comics that way. Smart move, I guess, although still a little chickenshit if you ask me. Bad guys are always more interesting, right?

My ex, Tasha, that bitch, was pretty hot, and I know she's really into the bad boy thing. She works as a receptionist at a Ford dealership. She was all about the sex. She had a reputation, but that didn't bother me. Not too bright – she'd flunked her year and done a victory lap, and still blown it, but I didn't give a shit – I wasn't looking to get married. It's funny, everybody just thought she was kind of dumb, but she played me pretty good. That took some smarts. A real survivor, that one. Her parents were definitely not the regular type for our school. They were very working-class. Real blue collar. I think they ate beans and rice for ten years just to send her there. She looked a little funky too, with pretty cheap clothes, but she had a killer body. She really stood out from everybody else, and they never let her forget it. Everybody ragged on her behind her back for being a slut, or a hillbilly, but she didn't give a shit. She hung with me pretty tight for a while, and the sex *was* great. I'd call her a whore and a slut and she loved it. I would swipe a credit card down her ass crack like in that Nelly video, *Tip Drill* – she laughed like crazy. She once answered the door wearing nothing but Saran Wrap. She was so hot – my little porn star. I always thought, you know, a girl who's that into sex, just into having fun, it was great. But then she went and betrayed me – I guess she lived up to her reputation. I thought we were really great together; she was a no-bullshit girl, and I just thought we were a good team. Man, was I wrong. I'm not saying she broke my heart or anything, fuck her, but I did feel pretty messed up about it. I just thought she was different from the rest ... but I was wrong.

But that's not why I did it. I know my family is going to catch a lot of shit about this now. I'm a monster. All those kids. My fellow students. The ones who I worked next to, who I shared laughs and joints and torments with, who teased and bullied me as I did them, who competed with me for status and acceptance. And all those wonderful teachers who taught me that God is dead, that each generation has fucked the planet over more and more, turning it into a superheated toilet, that we're killing off species at faster and faster rates, that we're heading for economic disaster, that our ideas of progress are false and destructive – those teachers with their stupid little games and tortures, how could I do this to them? I could lie and say I was really messed up, but really, I wasn't. I guess it wasn't that hard to cross the line from thinking some crazy shit to doing some crazy shit. Well, not for me anyway. And I'm gonna keep telling you, I never wanted to hurt anyone. That was Jeremy's idea. I know you want to hear about him – I want to lay this all out in my way, so hang tight. I'll get to him.

So, on with *The Shocking Inside Story of Teenage Madness!* Still no answers for you? Awww, what's wrong? Didn't you study for the test? You want me to *give* you the answers? How's this … About a year and a half back, I was on the fast track – climbing up the ladder to everlasting success. Like I said before, I was an "A" student. Scholarships lined up, university offers, it was all just perfect. So it's about six weeks before the end of the year, and everybody's starting to get even more uptight about their finals which are about four weeks away. It's after school and I'm in Mr. Nelson's room with about four other guys, going over some bitching physics assignment that *nobody* understands. As usual. Anyway, he gets a phone call and tells us he has to go outside to meet his wife to get whatever. He'll be back in five minutes. And he leaves. So, we're sitting there and I see he didn't lock down his computer.

His computer.

I can *see* he has the physics exam on it.

And the calculus exam.

And just about every other fucking exam in the world. I don't know, I just got up, took out my jump drive, and put it in the computer. And copied them. Just like that. Too easy. Too fast. Even now I'm not really sure why I did it. I mean, I probably would have done really well on the exams anyway. But I was thinking, this is my moment. I can do this because I can. I can rise above the rest because I can. Everybody in the room is just staring at me, and I just stare back like, yeah? It's like my *Ubermensch moment.* You know, everybody was thinking about doing it, but *I did it.* It would really lock in my scholarships, and I could hear my dad saying, *Be the best … be number one … it's about winning* … and that was it. None of the guys said anything. The girls … I just stared them down like a stone-cold killer. Nobody tried to stop me. I didn't feel guilty or bad about it, because, you know, everybody cheats. Shit, I went home that night and saw all these Wall Street guys getting *more* money after they'd fucked everybody else over. Tell me about fairness again please. Go big or go home. Everybody cheats, all the time. Here, or at university, and in business, sports, whatever. I just don't see the big deal. I can download anything I want, why can't I use somebody else's stuff? Use whatever advantage you can to get ahead. I mean, since *everybody* does it, how can it be stealing, right? I just did what others didn't have the guts to do. I don't know, maybe the only bad part was that I got caught.

When *that* happened, the principal and Mr. Nelson wasted no time.

"How could you do this?"

"Didn't you know you'd get caught?"

"How do you feel now?"

"Aren't you sorry you did this?"

What a bunch of stupid, sorry-ass questions! Was I supposed to answer these seriously? What's the point of saying things that everyone already knows the answer to? Was that supposed to make them feel more powerful, or me worse? I didn't say much, not because I was embarrassed, but because I didn't want them to think they got one over on me. I was a statue. I Robot. I wasn't going to give them an edge. They thought they're so smart? Seriously, if I search my feelings or whatever, I can't really say I felt that bad. About stealing the exams, I mean. I felt pretty shitty about getting caught. My dad had promised me a BMW Z4 if I got accepted to a university with a top scholarship. When I got busted, he just kept going on about getting caught – he didn't say too much about how wrong it was to cheat. One of his favourite sayings is, "Pigs get fat; hogs get slaughtered." I never could quite figure out what the difference between a pig and a hog is, and whenever I asked him about it, he'd just shrug or mumble something about being smart. Whatever.

Well, our principal, Mr. White (really, that's his name) really screwed me over. He called my parents in for a meeting – well, my mom, because my dad was away – and told her that I was going to lose my year, *and* get kicked out of the school. I don't know how much my mom bribed White – it must have been a truckload of cash, but at the end they agreed to put me on disciplinary intervention for the following year. This meant that they'd be watching me all the time. White figured he had me nailed – no other school would take me without the same thing happening, and my school had the best academic profile in the area of any private prep, so there it was. I was fucked. Then the scholarship rejections and deferred acceptance refusals started pouring in from all my universities. Now I was clusterfucked.

So anyway, all my so-called friends get to graduate, and I'm left holding the flaming shit bag. All those guys, they all started avoiding me like I had AIDS. A few other pals hung out, but I could tell they felt guilty, and they swore they hadn't ratted me out. I didn't believe them, and that still didn't change the fact of me being the only one who got busted. By the middle of the summer they were all disappearing, getting ready to go away to their universities. Everybody I knew would be ahead of me now. They'd lapped me, and it would be twice as hard to catch up. No matter what I did, I would always be looking ahead at them, farther up the track. They would always be crossing the finish line first, and I'd be in second place. Krystal, the bitch, never stopped riding me about it. Now she could really stick it to her brother. I was feeling pretty down. I went to talk to my dad about it, y'know, to try and feel better I suppose. He took me to his club. We had a steambath, and a massage. Played golf. Well, *he* played golf. I caddied, sort of. Drove the cart. We had a big dinner, and we drank some scotch. All he did was talk about how setbacks are opportunities seen in a different way, how I had to make the best of it. Like Forrest Gump, making lemonade out of lemons.

"Did Forrest Gump let his setbacks get him down? Now, *he* had problems you could complain about! But he didn't let those problems get to him!"

I told him that Forrest was a retard, but he just looked at me like he was trying, *really patiently*, to talk to a five year-old.

"He was mentally differentiated. But if a man with differences like those can overcome adversity, so can you!" I reminded him it was a Hollywood movie. He shrugged.

I asked him if he thought what I did was so bad. He just looked away, and then at me, hard. "Pigs get fat, son, hogs get slaughtered."

Forrest Gump is a stupid movie. The only part that was OK was the bit in Vietnam, but that didn't last too long. I don't see what's so inspirational about running across the country for no reason, and I really don't believe that any beautiful chick is going to fall in love with a retard. Even when she's dying. "Life is like a box of chocolates – you never know what you're going to get." Well, I got a piece of shit.

I went to talk to my mom, Lauren. She said that she remembered in the first two seasons of *Survivor* how Cirie Fields should have won at least one of the seasons. All the moves that Parvati took credit for in Micronesia? Eric giving up his idol? That was all Cirie's doing. By the time they got to the Heroes vs. Villains season, everybody was on to her, and she made a lot of mistakes, but she could manipulate people with such quiet ease, staying low, just pulling the strings through other people. Lauren says that Cirie has been a model for her business strategy, and that watching Cirie has helped her sell houses. She's been a true inspiration for her. I don't get it though. She ended up losing. Then my dad heard about Lauren's choice, and he said that Rob Mariano was clearly the best. He should have won the first All Stars tournament, totally dominating physically and with awesome social playing – even his opponents protected him. He could totally read the room, and could sit back and just do whatever was necessary to win. It was only his alliance with Tyson, who was stupid, which ruined his chances of winning in the second season and allowed Russell to win. Rob was a true leader, he could think multiple stages ahead, and he was really funny. *My* favourite would have to be Brian Heidik, who won the Thailand season. He totally dominated from the beginning to end. Some people say this made the Thailand season the worst ever, but they don't get it. Brian was a *machine*, man! Watching him was like watching Dexter play Survivor. Brian didn't have any hesitation about axing his own team members when it suited his purpose. Amazing. The guy is actually one of the wealthiest car salesmen in the country *and* an ex-softcore porn star. He's done it all! I figured he sounded better to me than Cirie or Rob Mariano, and this just made my mom and dad angry, and the two of them ended up arguing and forgetting I was even in the room.

It's really a mystery to me, the way people communicate. I mean, why don't they teach you *that* in school?

Maybe if I knew a little more about *that*, then I'd still have a girlfriend. Then again, seeing as how stuff has turned out, maybe not. Anyways, I guess I should tell you some more about Tasha. Like I said, she really fucked me over, I'll admit. You know, I guess I was pretty messed up about it, I mean, she really punked me, but in a way I have to thank her, because it helped me move to the next level, so, y'know .... It was like this. Me and her were lying around one time after getting it on, and it was four in the morning, and everything was dead quiet. I could hear her heart beating. She was kissing me, and I was trying to stay awake, because it really pissed her off when I fell asleep. She was stroking my face, and it all felt ... so safe, y'know? I was looking at her, and she had this little smile, and it was all so perfect. Nobody was judging me, I was just ... safe. I propped myself up on an elbow and I looked at her, and then it just came out –

"Have you ever been with a girl?" I said. She looked at me kind of funny, like, she really didn't know what to say, but not in a good way.

She said, "You mean have I fooled around with another girl?"

"Basically."

"Yeah," she says, just like that. "A couple of times. It was fun I guess, but it's not really my thing." Now, I'm starting to get turned on. She's smiling at me, 'cause she knows what's going on in my head. "You interested?"

"Fuck yeah," I say, like, obviously. But then her smile starts to fade, and she just says, "Nah, I'm not into it." I figure she's toying with me, you know, just cockteasing me, stringing me along.

"What's up with that? Why not? It would be so hot!"

"For you maybe," she says, and turns away. She turns back, "How about you?"

"How about me what?"

"Well, have you fooled around with any guys?"

Now I'm pissed, because I don't think that's too funny.

"What the fuck are you on about? Do I seem gay to you?" Now I'm thinking, I know I take awesome care of my frame – I work out seriously, and I can turn you on to some serious protein supplements – I'm pretty ripped, so maybe she's thinking I might swing with some fags, 'cause most of them look pretty cut to me.

"So, it's hot when I fooled around with some girls, but if you did it with another guy it would be weird?"

I'm just getting confused now, and a bit pissed. She's staring at me, and she's actually getting mad at me, I mean, really mad. Go figure. So I grab her and I figure a little loving will get her going in the right direction again. Angry sex is the best, right? She's wriggling and pushing me away, but I'm not giving up. I grab my phone – "You look so fucking hot," I say as I start to video her. I put it down and start in with her real seriously. It was pretty intense. She got into it – shit, by the end she was riding me like a rodeo star!

I figured that was it. I figured wrong. More on that in a sec.

So anyways, I started my make-up year as a model student. Oh sure, I figured I could really transform myself, y'know, make a new start and show everybody that I could be the best *even if I had to work for it myself*! No cheating, no bullshit. It started out OK – I was pulling down decent grades in all my subjects. I was feeling pretty good, even though everybody avoided me in the halls all the time. It didn't really get to me, at least not at first. I figured I could win them over if they saw I could do it the old-fashioned way.

In our English class Mr. Adams had us look at some poetry, and I really liked this one called "One Night." It was by Gottfried Benn. I'd never heard of the guy.

> One night, that no one knows
> Made out of mist, dampness and rain,
> In a place with no name,
> So unknown, so small, so out of the way,
>
> I saw the madness of all love and sorrow,
> The futility of desires and purposes,
> The theatrical on all sides,
> I saw how the hands had never been supported by God,
>
> Those hands, hot and unwashed, which want to caress you,
> Want to hold you, yet do not know
> How one should hold the other, on which stitches
> One must sew nets so they don't tear –

Ah, this mist, this coldness,
This falling away from all endurance,
From all bonds, faith, support, intimacy,
Ah, God – the gods! Dampness and shivering!

I don't know why I liked it. We talked about it in class. The weight of the world bearing down on us, amounting to what? I'm not going to go over all that. It just spoke to me somehow. I mean, this guy really had the meaninglessness of life pretty much nailed, right? I showed it to Tasha, and she said she didn't get it. I tried telling her about it more, but she just shrugged and said she didn't know. Then we fucked. But she took off right after, which was strange, because usually she liked to hang, and go a few more laps. Not this time. She said she had to be somewhere. I offered to give her a drive, but she turned me down, which was also weird. Now I was starting to get spooked. I start thinking she's looking to dump me, which is weird because chicks don't do that to me. It works the other way around, sure, but I figure, if she's that stupid, then it's her loss. Christ, I mean, she can't even get a stupid poem – how empty-headed can a chick be? I can do better, I know it. I've got the whole package right here! Can you see these abs? A full four-pack! Anyways, I'm thinking fuck it, and fuck her. Nobody blows me off. I make a few calls, even call a few of her girlfriends. Whatever.

I'm going to all my classes. On time. Doing all the work they told me to do.
I'm crunching all the numbers.
I'm writing down all the dates.
I'm memorizing all the names.
I'm repeating all the formulas.
I'm running. I'm jumping. I'm throwing.

Up.

How do you like that poem? Anyways, the more I tried to be good, the more they looked at me. Everybody. The juniors scurried away from me like terrified mice. They just clutched their books and looked away. The seniors whispered and smirked. It was like I had that scarlet letter on me, except this time it was a C for cheater. All I got from them was little strangled hellos and that was it. No one wanted to work with me. The teachers were no better. Little lectures and lots of notes in red pen, even when I did well. A couple of times I challenged some marks, and that just got me into long after-school arguments, so I gave up on that. A few visits to the vice-principal, Mr. McCreight. This guy looked like a zombie, I swear. Ten feet tall, skinny like a steel pole with gunmetal skin, a giant steel wool beard, and beady rat eyes. I'm pretty sure he had some fangs in there too.

"*We hope you are applying yourself. You know the penalty for another infraction.*" Yeah.

So I was taking a Philosophy class, and it was pretty cool. My teacher, Ms. Robertson, was telling us about Plato's Cave. Sounds like a cool club to me, but Ms. Robertson said that it's this theory that we're all living in a metaphorical cave. See, Plato said that we are chained in this cave facing the back, so all we see are shadows of the world outside. But since that's all we've ever seen, we think that the shadows are the real stuff of life. So, we live in a world of illusions. I'm kind of thinking I know how he felt. We watched *The Matrix* in class, and there it was, exactly like Plato said. Ms. Robertson also told us how it's also like the Bible, but I don't really give a shit about that. Jesus!? Whatever. But, you know, illusions are really lies, right? And the more I looked around, the more of them I saw.

I could tell that things with Tasha were kind of going bad. I couldn't believe it had anything to do with me asking about her and other girls. I decided to confront her about it. I mean, if she wanted to split with me, OK, too bad for her, but I wanted to be sure. I arranged to meet her at the mall, I figured, a neutral space for us to talk. Plus, we could go shopping. We're sitting in the food court, but she's on another planet. I mean, I even ask her if she's high, and she gets pissed off. I thought it was a reasonable question, because she's looking everywhere but at me, and one leg is bobbing up and down like she's doing squats or something. Real hyper.

She says, "I'm thinking of seeing someone else."

I can't believe it. I figure I'll make a joke out of it.

I say, "What's her name?"

"Not funny."

"C'mon, why so serious?"

"Didn't you hear me? I think it's time for a change."

I can't believe I'm hearing this.

"You're fucking with me, right? I'm sorry about the lesbo thing."

"What is your problem?"

"What is *my* problem? Really? You're the one with the problem. Maybe you really do chicks."

"And maybe you do guys."

Now I'm thinking, really, what is up with this crazy bitch?

"You think I'd do guys? Me, doing guys? I just want to be clear here. You're saying – I fuck guys. Right? You're saying I'm gay? I like guys? Are you out of your fucking mind?"

She's staring at me, like I'm a million miles away already.

Then this look comes into her eyes ... no, it's like a whole new person is sitting there in front of me ... she sucks in this deep breath, and then she stares at me like she's looking into the distance, somewhere behind me. I actually turn around for a second because I think she's looking past me, but there's no one behind me that I recognize. I turn back around and she's got this little smile on her face.

"You're really such a kid."

"What …?"

"You're just really a little boy. I didn't see it before. You and your toys and all your using of … everything. You're a …"

"Fuck you," I say, and I'll admit, it probably wasn't my best line, but then I followed up with –

"Who the fuck are you to tell me anything? You didn't even finish high school. You're a slut-retary in a car dealership and you –"

– which is when I get a cappuccino frappe deluxe thrown in my face, and she stomps off. All I hear through the foam is her cursing, and saying I'll be sorry. For what, I wonder?

I really don't get the whole love thing. I mean, what is it exactly? Is it just liking someone more than you usually do? And what's the point if you end up just getting bored like my parents are? I don't see how it's worth it. I think it might be better to just feel the same about everything, you know, don't be an asshole or anything, but don't go crazy and run around singing about how much you love someone. You ever hear this band The Mountain Goats? A lot of the songs are about how sad life is and the lead singer is kind of a loser, but he's really smart actually and his songs are pretty cool. Most pop songs are all about how great love is, even when they're trying to be cool or tough. Not these guys. They lay it out. This love stuff hurts, and it will fuck you up. Period. I was listening to this one called "Love Love Love." Check it out:

Raskolnikov felt sick
But he couldn't say why
When he saw his face reflected
In his victim's twinkling eye
Some things you do for money
And some you'll do for fun
But the things you do for love
Are gonna come back to you one by one

So, I google Raskolnikov and it turns out he's a character is this super-famous Russian novel from back in the day. So it's about a guy who kills an old lady and her sister just to see if he can, and he gets all messed up with guilt about it, but he doesn't want to turn himself in, and then he does, and then he doesn't, and he falls in love with a prostitute, and he struggles with confessing for forever before he finally does cave in. So, I'm listening to this song, and I think I get it. This guy feels sick because he feels guilty, but he *can't admit to himself* that he feels that way. And Wikipedia said he did it because he was trying to prove to himself that he *could* do it, just like the guys in *Rope*, just like Nietzsche said. But Raskolnikov is all torn up about it, so he realizes he's *not* the Superman type, and that tears him up even more. And I think the song here is saying that in the end love will make us do *really* stupid things, and we can't escape that. Maybe it's worked out differently for you, and love is all great for you. Good luck with that. I just wish for me I could feel some of the really good things, because it sure feels really fucked up stupid right now.

I figured that was it for me and Tasha. Not quite. Oh no.

A couple days later I wake up and I've got like ... hundreds of tweets all about how I'm a fag and I suck cock and all sorts of shit. I mean, there's tons of them ... I can't scroll through them all … I don't recognize most of them. I'm just sitting there, and it feels like I can't even get out of bed. It's like my phone is suddenly pushing me back down into the bed, and I can't raise my body up. Everything goes quiet. There's a lot of nasty shit there … really sick stuff. Then I see one has a link. I click it.

There I am.

In my room.

I'm walking around, naked.

And you can hear my voice.

"I fuck guys."

"I'm gay."

"I like guys."

It's my voice. You don't see me saying it, but you hear it.

What the fuck?

I look at my email and see that my video of me and Tasha fucking was emailed to her. She took my phone … when I wasn't looking or around … and she … she …

Oh fuck.

I'm thinking, I'm going to kill her, right? I mean, *kill* her. But everybody knows we've been together, and so the cops will target me for sure. Then I'm thinking, I could get somebody else to do it, but, y'know, could I trust them to really do it? And what if they ratted me out, or were caught and broke it to the cops? I mean, it all pointed back to me, right?

I didn't know what to do. I could go to the cops and tell them what she did. And then there'd be an extra big PUSSY sign that I could wear next to the FAG one. I couldn't do that. And then I realized, there's nothing I could do. I was just gonna have to tough it out.

It was the end of my first term. My marks were not great, but OK. Now I had to deal with this. I thought it was bad before with people avoiding me? Holy shit. Everywhere I went, they stared. I heard the whispers, which sometimes weren't whispers at all. My locker got tagged. I got into a couple of fights, not *at* school of course. I dreaded turning on my phone or my computer. It was relentless. Everybody wanted me gone, or worse, I don't know. It got so I gave up even trying to fight back. It took so much energy … I just got so tired. Everything was grey, and it felt like I was walking around with lead boots. Even the air felt thick. It was hard to even open my eyes in the morning. I didn't care anymore. Then it was like, suddenly I actually started getting *into* it. *That's right* you bastards! Everything started to take on this hard edge. I stared them all down. Everything had this little whining, high-pitched sound behind it. I'd show them. Stay away from me, because I don't *need* anyone anyway. I would show everybody that I was going to be a winner and I could do it without anybody, and that was just fine. And I'd make them all pay. Fuck all of you. You ever see this movie called *Carrie*? It's pretty wild. It's about this kid who's got telekinetic powers – she can move stuff and make things happen, and her mom is this really fucked up Jesus freak, and all the kids make fun of her at school. She's a total loner, and this one kid pulls off a plan to humiliate her at the prom by pouring a whole bucket of blood on top of her, but Carrie gets revenge by burning the whole town down after nuking the whole prom. Wild. After I saw it I read the Stephen King novel – I think it's fantastic. It really gets you into the head of a kid who feels all alone, and how fucked up other kids can be. Now that I think of it, it's kind of like what I wanted to do. Well, I guess it *is* what I did. Me and Carrie White – *"They're all gonna laugh at you!"* Not any more.

So I spent my days walking around school like Donnie Darko, you know? Like, I'm wandering in this other reality, and I'm getting a bad feeling about it all. Then this new student arrived from nowhere in the middle of the year. That's usually not a good sign, because, unless you moved from another city, why would you be changing schools, right? So, whatever, I didn't pay him much attention at first, but I *was* kind of curious, because he looked pretty cool.

Kind of like me, actually.

He was a big guy, around 6 feet, sandy blond hair (shorter than mine), good body (pretty cut), and well-dressed – I mean, none of that baggy-ass prison hip-hop shit. This guy had a great motorcycle jacket, some cool, simple T-shirts, black jeans and black lace-up boots. Nice. Guy's name was Jeremy Anderson. I asked him why he transferred to our school, and all he said was, "Because the last one was full of losers." That's it. Fair enough. I could respect that. I mean, I guess it sounded rough, but he didn't come off that way. Just, y'know, totally straight-up. Not angry, just cool. He'd just look at you like he had this secret or something, and he wasn't going to give it up, at least not yet; he didn't push you away either. He just … seemed … so confident. Like me, I figured. Like Harper. A few kids started to try and hang out with him, but he didn't seem interested. They'd be showing him some new games, and he'd be like, whatever. Bored. I wanted to get to know this guy.

And then Harper showed up. Harper, my big bro. Come back to see his little brother? I got the feeling that Lauren called him to come and give me a pep talk, but he said he just flew in to see everybody because "it's been too long." At first I wanted to tell him to fuck off, whatever, but I knew that I was really happy to see him. I always really liked Harper because he was always so cool and so successful. He did great at anything he wanted to do, and he made it seem easy. I don't think I ever remember him not smiling. Is that a little weird or what? When we were kids, it almost seemed half the time that *he* was my dad. He gave me cool books, Carlos Castaneda and Hunter Thompson. He'd always include me in stuff that he and his friends were doing. He took me to a porno theatre – an actual theatre where they showed porno – I couldn't believe it! I mean, I'd seen porn, but not in a movie theatre. It was weird being in a room with other guys watching this stuff – pretty gross really. I mean, seriously, porn should really be seen alone.

He introduced me to grass when I was about thirteen, booze before that. He'd take me hiking with him, we'd drive out to the edge of the city and we'd kick around in the construction sites and abandoned factories there. He had this great .22 rifle, and we'd go shooting out windows in the building projects. I remember this one time I told him I wanted to shoot a bird. He looked at me all cool. "Oh yeah? You want to be the big hunter?" He handed me the rifle and pointed up at a sparrow up in the tall branches of some spindly old tree. It was way up there. I aimed up at it, but it was right above me, so it was hard to hold the rifle steady, y'know? So he reached around me, helping me hold it. Me and him, together. I looked up at that little thing, and gently squeezed the trigger, just like he taught me. At first I didn't think I hit it, because it fluttered like it was going to take off. But then it fell, and I could see it fall and hit the branches below it, and it kept falling, in slow motion, falling, fluttering, falling, until it finally got caught in some branches with us standing right below it. It was just a few feet above our heads. And I heard a drip sound. I looked down at my feet and there was a spot of blood. It was bright red, just dripping on my boot. I felt kind of queasy, kind of sick actually. I couldn't say anything. I looked at him, and he just took the gun from me. "That's shooting a bird," is all he said. I threw away my boots. I thought that would be the last time I ever killed anything.

So I came home from school and there he was, just sitting in the kitchen, tearing into a huge salad, drinking a glass of wine, and reading the *New Yorker*. Man, I just look at that magazine and fall asleep. I don't get it. He looked totally comfortable there, like he owned the place and just got home from work. He looked up at me and smiled, lifting his glass, taking a sip – cool as cool. He just said something like, "What's up?" or "What's going on?" Just like that. I stared at him for a second, and then I couldn't help myself, I ran over to him and he gave me a hug, like I was a little kid or something. At that moment I felt that everything was going to be OK with me. He told me that he heard about me getting busted. Then I told him about the video getting around, and he held up his hand and told me to stop. I looked at him, waiting to hear what he had to say. He just smiled. I told him what Dad said about making the best of a bad situation. He nodded. I asked him what I should do. First he told me that I was stupid to make the video in the first place, and even stupider to leave my phone lying around unlocked.

"You got to get tighter with your shit." Whatever that meant. He just told me to do what I had to do. I told him that's not a big help. He looked at me all funny, as if I'd just said something in another language. He took a deep breath, and I'll never forget this, because it felt so right when I heard it. He looked at me, real serious now, kind of leaning in to me and holding me with his stare, those golden eyes nailing me down to the floor. He said, "Make them notice you. Make them see you." That was it. He smiled, and went back to his salad, leaving me standing there like a waiter picking up the cheque. Then his phone rang, and that was it.

He hung around for a few more days, but most of it was spent on the phone. I didn't know why he came home really. I mean, I'm glad he did, because we got to hang and play some games. We didn't talk much more. He told me he was doing great. He had a couple of girlfriends in L.A. and he said I should come out and visit him when I graduated. I asked him if he could hook me up with a job, but he shook his head and said I had to figure out what I really wanted to do. I said I just wanted to be doing what he was doing, and we could be like a team. He laughed and said that wasn't going to happen. I told him he was being real cold to me. He just kept laughing and told me to grow up. He said that just trying to copy him was a pussy thing to do, and everybody would know it. Man, I didn't get it. One minute he was being all cool with me, then the next he was being this cold fucker, like my dad. You know that Kanye West rap "Big Brother"? It's all about how Kanye is exploring his feelings about Jay-Z, how competitive they are, and how one second he loves the guy and the next second he's totally dissing him? That is kind of like how I see me and Harper. I'm not sure if I would be Kanye and Harper would be Jay-Z, maybe it's the other way around, but I don't think so. Yeah, I think I'm like Kanye and he's Jay-Z. It's complicated.

Anyways, I'm sitting in class, counting air molecules until it's time to take off, and suddenly I get this weird queasy feeling, and I turn in my seat and I see that Jeremy is totally staring at me. Not staring like checking me out, but just, like gazing at me with this smug smile on his face. I'm about to tell him to fuck off, right there in class, but then I see him motion to his ear, and he nods at me. I realize he's scoped out the single ear-bud going with my iPhone. I always kept it nicely hidden, tucked around the ear, under hair, high collar, with good hand cover whenever the teacher did a walk-around (which was pretty much never). I'd say most of the kids used their phones during class, but so many of them did it sloppily and got busted. Of course, *now* they're allowing it in some classes – great – after I'd spent five years getting busted for it! Whatever. Jeremy was impressed. Later he came up to me and asked me what I was listening to. I threw him a few recent faves – Peaking Lights, EMA, Gang Gang Dance, I Break Horses – I'm really into a lot of psychedelic, trance stuff, a lot of dub – and I could tell he was impressed. He asked me if I'd checked out any I-Dosing, and I figured I'd be honest and say no. He gave me a big smile and told me it was really cool. There's these internet sites that transmit sound frequencies – binaural beats and ambient frequencies, and you download MP3 files and listen to them for an hour or whatever and you can get high. Digital drugs. There's different ones and different highs that you can get. The binaural beats are frequencies that are really close together but not quite identical, and when you listen to them with lots of bass through good headphones, your brain tries to sync its own frequencies to that of the track, and it sort of alters your state of mind. So, Jeremy shows me a list of different frequencies and what they do, like, release endorphins, and enkephalins, and serotonin, and you get everything from stress release to total visualizations, like with acid.

I *had to* check this out, right? So, he came over and I'd already found a couple of sites for downloads. The files were all around five bucks, so I downloaded a few with names like LSD-25, Orgasm, and MDMA. Stuff I was familiar with, right? I wasn't too interested in Weight Loss or Active Relaxation. So, we were in my basement, nobody else home, we had superior

Sennheiser headphones, and a beanbag chair each. A bottle of water, lights down, off we went. Annnnnnddd … – nothing. Like, fuck all. An hour of fuzz and occasional beats, and I *wanted* to be stoned, I *wanted* to say that I was soooo fucked up, but the truth was, zilch. I was looking at Jeremy and he was looking at me, and I shrugged. He cracked up laughing. He said, "Yeah, it's bullshit, but you should try it after a few joints or some E." I asked him if that didn't sort of refute the whole point of the thing, and he just shrugged. And cracked up again. Then he pulled out a number and we lit up.

Different story then.

A few days later I'm leaving school and there's like four guys hanging out at the parking lot, and I could tell right away things weren't cool. They're standing there, leaning against a couple of cars, but I could just see an edge, some kind of wired, shaky vibe to them. They were probably jacked. I figured I'd just be totally cool and walk past them, but as soon as I got to them, they block my path. In a second I'm surrounded. So fucking cliché, but I had to admit I was worried. I could see they were jacked – little tiny pinholes for pupils, the smell of sour sweat, yeah, they were flying. They start to yammer away at me – something about being a loser, being a fag, being a cheater – this tired list goes on – I can barely make sense out of them – for some reason I flash to an image of hyenas circling a prey – and I know with this sinking, cold feeling in my gut that I'm going to have to fight my way out of this. They're backing me up against one of the cars. Then, behind them, back at the school doors, I see Jeremy walking out. I'm thinking of calling out to him, but that would just pussify me more. But I send out a silent one, for sure. Help a brother out, y'know? No, more like, please save my ass. And that was it. I see him scope us out, and real silent and casual, like a dark cloud whipped by the wind, I see him scudder across the parking lot – one second he's back there by the doors – then he's bending down and picking up a fist-sized rock – and then he's right behind them, his hand flying in a blur to bring the rock smashing against the cheek of the guy nearest him. This guy made the mistake of turning as he heard Jeremy at the last second, exposing his mouth to two pounds of stone at the end of a whipping arm – I saw teeth flying out as his head snapped back. He goes down like a dropped brick. His buddies are frozen – seriously, and it's almost funny, except Jeremy doesn't think so. With the same movement he brings his rock-holding hand backwards across the guy next to Broken Mouth, a little higher this time, connecting with the dude's nose. I hear this wet crack and blood just pours out of it, like a fountain. I'm frozen this whole time; I mean, I want to move, but it's like I don't have time for it somehow. The other two guys just turn and run, and Broken Nose grabs Broken Mouth and they stagger after their pals. Jeremy drops the rock and turns around, watching them stagger off.

I start to stutter thanks but he just waves a hand at me like it's no biggie.

"Nothing is more pussy than an unfair fight. You OK?"

I nod. He gives my shoulder a squeeze.

"I gotta take off. I suggest you do the same. They won't make any more shit. You got a ride?"

I nod the other way. He seems to scowl at me, like, 'what kind of loser takes the bus?' "C'mon." He reaches behind me – I'm standing next to his car.

"Actually, I beat those fuckers because they were hanging by my ride." And sure enough, he walks slowly around the car to check it out. I laugh. "You think that's funny?" My laugh dies in my throat.

We get in. It was a sweet ride – a BMW Z4 – the same car I wanted. Loaded. Everything about that car is just … the ultimate. A lean, luxurious driving machine, y'know? Like, you can just *sense* the power of the thing. And Jeremy, he just seems born into that car … I mean, he looked – I remember thinking … he looked like he was *part of it*, like … actually part of the car. Like, in a good way – a finely tuned machine, everything just humming and cool. Anyways, I start thanking him again, and I try and make a joke like, 'I was just about to smash that guy in his fist with my face …' but it dies in my throat. We both know I was dead meat. He just waves me off. Then he says, "What are you going to do?" I'm a bit confused – does he mean the guys who swarmed me? He shrugs.

"When are you going to take charge?"

Now I really don't know what he's talking about.

"Look …," he says, gunning the engine as if he's getting annoyed, "you've gotten busted for cheating – no, stealing an exam. You've gotten punked for being a fag, which I know is bullshit but that doesn't matter, and now I save your ass from getting trashed. That's three strikes. Shit, I just got here, and it looks pretty bad from where I'm sitting."

Now I shrug. He chuckles. Who chuckles? Like, really? Chuckling?

"Look man, you don't get to shrug anymore. I can shrug. I can not give a shit, but you … you're sinking fast. You have to man up. Seriously. I've seen great guys get fucked up with their shit and it can ruin them. You're getting very close."

I give him my best cool look. "I can handle it."

"Really? When is that supposed to happen? 'Cause right now, I'm just seeing a pussy. And so is everybody else. You might have been hot shit once upon a time, but that ship has sailed, man. What are you going to do?"

I don't know what to say. We're gliding along, and suddenly it feels like I'm being pulled somewhere, like I'm not even in a car, but just … being pulled towards a cliff or a wall or some kind of bad fucking mojo batshit bullshit ending to a movie I didn't even want to be in. How did I become such a fuckup? I'm supposed to be *the man*! And then I say it …

"I don't know what I'm gonna do."

"That's it? You don't know? That's pretty sad, man. '*I don't know, mommy*'" –

And all of a sudden I want to smash the smug right off of his face.

"Why the fuck should you care? Who the fuck do you think you are anyways?" I'm shouting now, trying not to sound panicked, just really fucking angry.

The car comes to a soft, gliding stop. We're in front of my house. He turns to me.

"Me? I'm your only friend in the world. I'm the guy that's going to help you win." I remember getting out of that car and thinking, 'maybe this is going to be my time now' … y'know? Maybe this guy is going to help me out.

I was starting to hang out more with Jeremy. He seemed to be gliding along, and doing well, and nothing seemed like too much of an effort for him. The girls liked him, he had money, and he was just … so … cool. He really reminded me of Harper. It's like nothing touched him, or stuck to him that he didn't want to. I never actually saw him do any work, but it got done anyway. I knew he was dealing a little bit – I'd seen him make a few underhand passes in the food court near the school. It was weed mostly, but I'd seen some pills, probably E. No biggie to me.

I asked Jeremy if I could get in on a little selling, y'know, just to help him out. I mean, I knew kids that probably might have been a bit freaked out by him or whatever, but he didn't go for it. He told me he was doing just fine, and I guess he was. I was getting kinda curious about him, y'know, wanting to know more about him, or maybe just hang out more with him, but he was always keeping me off-balance in a way. Like, I'd be texting him, and then all of a sudden he wouldn't reply. For the whole day. Then he'd be back, no explanation. Or, I'd be leaving my house to go to school, and he'd just be waiting in his car, right outside. It could even be a bit creepy I guess, although I didn't think about it too much at the time. Some of the kids started a nickname for him ... The Shroud. I guess it fit. Once we started to hang out, I'd try asking him about his family. He didn't say much about his parents at all. At first I thought that was weird. I'd heard that his dad was actually on some prison farm somewhere on a big investment fraud bust, and that he had millions hidden in some offshore accounts, but I wasn't going to ask Jeremy about *that*. His mom remarried to some lawyer, I think it was the guy that represented his dad in court. Ouch. Whenever I mentioned anything about his family, he just said he was raised by wolves, and then adopted into civilization. I got the message. I figured that's OK, since I didn't really care or anything. I knew they were loaded – what else did you need to know, right? He didn't get that car dealing grass.

I never went to his place, which I guess is kinda weird. He told me he had moved with his mom into some upscale condo downtown, even though they had a house, and she was selling it and looking for another. I guess she was into the flipping thing too, or maybe she had to sell it to pay for his old man's legal bills or whatever. I met her once, when he was dropping her off somewhere. He pulled up and she got out of the car, and man, I know it sounds a little weird but she looked pretty hot. I mean, you're not supposed to say that about a pal's mom, but she was pretty smokin'. And what was even weirder was that I could have sworn that she gave me the eye when she said hi. I mean, I don't see how that can be in my head, right? But she really did kind of linger on that hello with a smile that just seemed a bit … much. Of course, it all kind of made sense to me later.

So anyways, things were not going so great for me at school. You'd think the teachers would be all on my side, but not so. I mean, I got some sympathy from them at first, but they kept riding me about what I was saying. Telling me that I needed to learn about sensitivity and equal rights and stuff. Meanwhile it's my ass up there everybody is laughing at. Fuck all of you.

I guess I should say that not *all* the teachers at my school are uptight pricks. There was this one, Mr. Polland, who seemed pretty cool. He was our Media Studies teacher. He was this ex-hippie who belonged to a farm commune that raised emus. I shit you not. Emus are like ostriches if you didn't know. Whatever. He wore dark glasses *in class when we watched movies*! Anyway, it was a cool class. Basically we sat around and discussed videos and songs and stuff, and then we got to make our own. Actually, Polland assigned a project where we had to track some kind of trend in popular culture. I chose violence in movies and videogames. Go with what you know, right? That was what this video diary was supposed to be about actually, before, well, before things happened. Polland showed us some wild stuff too, lots of older movies which were really cool once you got past how scratchy and shitty-looking some of them were. He showed us this *really old* movie from the 60's – *Zabriskie Point* – I slept through most of it, whatever, but at the end there's this chick who just stares at this big luxury home up on a cliff, and the thing explodes over and over for like five minutes. All these different angles, and then all the debris floating down in slo-mo, and you've got this Pink Floyd music going and it's totally trippy. That is just pretty fucking great if you ask me. There's something that's just so cool about watching things fall apart, right? Check it out.

Anyway, Polland saw that I was pretty bummed about everybody picking on me, and I had started to skip his classes. So he cornered me and just said, "What did I ever do to you to make you treat me so disrespectfully?" I stared at him, like, what the fuck? *I'm* the one who's feeling bad! So he said that he hadn't seen me in class, and he went out a few nights ago in the pouring rain to buy this DVD about the 9/11 conspiracy that he thought I'd be into, and now I wasn't even bothering to come to class. His feelings were hurt! Can you believe it? He just shook his head, like "no respect man, no respect" and then he *gave* the DVD to me. And walked away. That was it. So I figured, OK, I'll go back to class.

So I went back there, and Polland was really paying attention to me, which seemed cool. I didn't really get it, 'cause he really seemed pretty weird to me, I mean, with all the farmer-Bob thing. He once asked me to hang back after class, and I figured I'm in some shit, although I have no idea what for. Instead, he just sits down with me and starts to ask me what I'm gonna do when I graduate. Nobody had even used *that* word in conversation with me this year. I'm looking at him like, I dunno, make as much cash as I can as fast as I can, hustling whatever I can. I remember, he just looked at me with this sad kind of expression, and told me I could do way better. Now, I didn't know what he meant, 'cause really, what could be better than that, right? He starts in talking about how I could really make a difference in the world, about what morality is and how some people can lead others down different paths, and how I could be a leader if I wanted to, and *still* make money at it but do it by being ethical, or good.

I told him I thought that was horseshit.

He laughed at me, which I didn't expect. He said there was a lot about the world that I didn't know about, and that you have to peel away at the truth to get to it. That's why he bought me that DVD. He said for instance that most people think anybody who questioned anything about the economic structure or anything like 9/11 was either a fanatic or just nuts. And the more you asked questions about it, the more nuts they think you were. I don't know, even though I thought he was kinda crazy, I started to like this guy. At least he was different from the rest. He showed me all kinds of documentaries, some in class, and some he lent to me. They were about different kinds of government corruption and conspiracies. Like the whole way the stock market is organized, a small group of traders always make money, even when they deliberately set out to rip people off, but most ordinary people stand to lose their life savings, or how even something small like the circuitry in my phone is made from this mineral called Coltan, which is mined in the Congo, and the army there is forcing their people to mine it, and raping and killing them if they don't cooperate, so basically your phone is filled with blood. Wow. I hope somebody gets on that, because, you know, I really need my phone. It's not that I'm trying to avoid really doing something about that. I mean, what am I supposed to do? Polland said I could start a petition or a letter campaign to the government, but you know, give me a break. As if that's going to work. I think I'd rather try to work on something smaller, maybe climate change or child slavery, but cellphones? I don't think so. I mean, when Polland went on about corporate brainwashing, and all that conspiracy stuff, I got it, I really did. But I don't see what we can do about it really. And besides, even if we did overthrow all the big bad corporations and change all the laws, they'd still find a way around them. It's what they do. And besides, I still want to be rich.

Mr. Polland was OK. Seems he was kind of a loner in the school. Kind of like me. Except that he was a little weird. Seems like a lot of the other teachers weren't too crazy about his style. I mean, he was really nice to all the students, and super laid-back. I think the conspiracy thing had a lot of the other teachers spooked. Or maybe it was the hippie thing. I mean, he could have probably used a haircut, because the Jesus hair was not a good look for him. But, y'know, in a weird way, the whole Farmer Bob thing was kind of cool *for a teacher* because it was like a big *fuck you* to all the other teachers. I mean, cheap polyester leisure suits and sweatpants get tired real fast, y'know? He kept loaning me books about different secret conspiracies, like Area 51 and Roswell, which are about real UFO sightings and landings and cover-ups, and The Bilderberg Group, which is this group of super elite businessmen and politicians who meet in secret every year to discuss world domination – I'm pretty sure my dad is in on that. I showed Polland a couple of videogames that are about this stuff too. The *Deus Ex* series is, like, totally excellent. The first one came out about ten years ago, and it won all kinds of awards for Best Game. Basically, it's a first-person shooter game, about this guy JC Denton, who works for the United Nations Anti-Terrorist Coalition in 2052, and he gets in real deep with conspiracies for world domination, with the Majestic 12, the Illuminati, and the Hong Kong Triads. It's pretty intense. There's all kinds of clues in it with references to Shakespeare and science-fiction books and stuff.

I showed this to Polland and he talked to me about all the literary aspects of the games. He gave me this book, called *Trading with the Enemy*, which is all about how American industrialists did business with the Nazis during World War II. Then he gave me another one called *Crossing the Rubicon – The Decline of the American Empire at the End of the Age of Oil.* It shows how 9/11 was created by the government as part of a larger plan to maintain control of the world economy now that Peak Oil has been reached, which is the fact that we are now running out of oil. The CIA is in on this, and Wall Street banks, and drug trafficking all over the world.

I'll admit it, I was really getting into these books. I mean, I always enjoyed the games to just kick back with, but I never really gave these ideas any real thought. But these books … they really made me think again. Don't get me wrong, I am still all about making it in a capitalist world. It just felt great to be in on something that felt like a new truth, something that felt like it had been withheld from me forever. I was in on it now. And it felt great that I'd made a friend with a teacher, which I never thought could ever happen.

So I'm talking about Polland to Jeremy, and he just looks at me like I'm high. He tells me that Polland is just playing me like teachers will do. I tell him I don't know what he's talking about. He says that teachers will try and get to you to manipulate you into thinking like they want you to. All that stuff about learning to think for yourself is really bullshit, because *they* are the system, and it's just a clever way of making you fall into line. I'm telling Jeremy that I didn't know, it felt pretty good to me the way Polland was giving me stuff to check out, and talking about stuff I liked, and he seemed really laid back and never put me down. Jeremy just looked at me and said, "He's good at it." I told him I just didn't know, and he said, "Trust me, he's just trying to mindfuck you."

I let it go for a bit, and I put a little space between me and Polland, you know, just to see how he'd react? See if Jeremy was right? The next time Polland tells me about a cool book I should check out, I tell him I have enough to read right now. He shrugs and says, "Sure," but a week later he mentions this movie he saw, and then another, and it seems to me that he's getting more desperate each time I brush him off. So then I'm thinking, yeah, fuck, maybe this is weird y'know? Polland can tell I'm pulling back, and he's looking at me weirdly. He asks me to hang back after class again, and this time he starts asking me if everything is OK. I tell him sure, and then he says he's definitely noticed that I'm not checking out anything he's telling me about. I shrug and say whatever, and ask if there's anything else he wants to talk to me about. He says no. I ask him if I can go and he just looks at me and says I don't need his permission to leave. So I do.

A week later Polland is called out of class. There's another teacher ready to take over the class. He never comes back. Supposedly they found some weed in his car. It seemed bizarre to me that he'd be that stupid, but you know, if you're baked enough, maybe you do something dumb. Hippies, man. Jeremy just shrugged and said, "I told you so." I looked at him like, 'What are you talkin' about? You said he was trying to mindfuck me, but dealing grass?' He pulls me close and says, "I'm just looking out for you, man."

I missed Polland, even if he was a flake. I didn't put it together then, even though it was right in front of me. I mean, why would Polland be dealing right out of school? Why would he have it in his car? Like, that's just stupid, even for a teacher! I just remember thinking, you know, this guy said he was all about uncovering the truth about stuff, and looking beyond what you're just told, and all that. And then it turns out that he's hustling just like everybody else, trying to just get his piece any way he can. I mean, I don't blame him for that, but he lied to me. I mean, shit, I was all *about* the hustle, but he could have been upfront with me. The one guy I thought was cool – other than Jeremy – turned out to be just like all the rest. Instead, he was just a little lying bitch like everybody else. That's what I thought at the time.

So anyway, life was shitty, but I was trying to be a soldier about it all, y'know? Whatever doesn't kill me makes me stronger, right? I still had Jeremy.

So I remembered having this dream a few nights later and it scared the shit out of me. I was in the hallway upstairs, and I was playing with our dog, Kahlua. I was younger, around six or seven I guess. So I was playing fetch with something up in the hall with him, throwing a dog toy or whatever. And suddenly he stopped at the other end of the hall and started barking at something. Weird, even for him. So I went to see what he was looking at, and there was this snake coiling along the floor towards him. It had wild colours on it, and it was hissing, and I knew it was poisonous. I grabbed the dog and started running down the hall, but he wriggled out of my arms and went running back towards it. Suddenly there was a mattress leaning up against the wall, and I grabbed the dog and flung the mattress down on top of the snake. I climbed on top of the mattress with the dog, and we could see the snake wriggling underneath it. The dog was barking like crazy, and I was trying to hold on to him. The whole floor was shifting now, like we were on water or something, and I looked up and there was snakes coming out of all the doors, wriggling down the hall towards us. I'm crying out for my mom and my dad, but nobody came. I screamed. That's it.

I couldn't figure out what the hell this dream was telling me. I certainly didn't want any snakes, fuck you very much, and I didn't even know what the hell I would be repressing, because I'm a guy who always speaks his mind, so that's that, right? Jeremy said it had something to do with my parents, but that I had to figure out what that might be. He was starting to sound a bit like Harper here, or that shrink, so I just decided to give it a pass. But it still freaks me out to think about it.

I was hanging out a few days later with Jeremy, and I told him about this dream, because it was *still* freaking me out. He looked at me with that "I can see through you" look and said that your dreams reveal something about you that you are trying to repress, or something that you really want. I asked him where he learned that, and he just said, "My case worker." Just like that. Like, "*it ain't no thang.*" I wanted to ask him what that was about, but I didn't. Not cool. I figured I'd let him tell me if he wanted to. I guess he could tell that I was kind of jonesing to find out. He waits a few days. He calls me up, "Hey bud, let's go for a ride." He liked to cruise around, smoking fatties and such, and just shooting the shit. So we're driving and he asked me if I wanted to drive. I couldn't believe it. I mean, I knew how much that car meant to him, and he was gonna let me drive? Shit! So he pulled over and we switched. Oh man, that was a sweet ride. It was like that engine was just part of me, y'know? I just touched the gas and it leapt like a lion with a stick up its ass! It was a tight ride, and Jeremy could see how much I was getting off on it. We're stopped at a light and he just says, like he's giving directions, "I have to see a case worker every week."

I don't know what to say. I mean, what do you say to that? I just mumbled something like, 'What's that about?'

"Just some shit that I got into a while back. I was rolling with a crew of older guys, some real hustlers, and some of it got real, and we got clipped." I'm looking at him and I'm too embarrassed to say like, 'what are you talking about, 'cause I have no idea' but I don't because I figure I'll look stupid. So I just nod like I get it. It sounds pretty heavy. He tells me it had to do with trying to sell some pills, and that he was the guy that moved the stuff through a whole network of schools. I couldn't believe there was that much money involved, but he told me, a few buildings with a thousand rich kids in each, it was pretty sweet. Anyways, he didn't get caught with the stuff, but there was somebody who rolled on him and he was brought in to the cops and eventually got moved to a new school – mine. "Of course, I got off with no big deal, I just have to check in with this fucknuts once a week and tell him about how well I'm adjusting to my new setting and working hard to acclimatize myself to new learning goals." Now I really am lost, and so help me, I can't help it – I start to laugh, and he's laughing too. Then he says, "You wanna meet some of these guys? They're real players. They could set you straight." Now I can't help but ask what the fuck that means. "Just … you know … help you out a bit." He tells me to pull over. Ride's done for now.

We were riding around one night, and suddenly he floored it way out on the fringe of town. There was nothing out there but old factories and gravel pits. Cement factories, railroad tracks, auto body shops. We smoked a fat rollie, got the tunes pumping, the sun was setting, life was good. He turned to me with a big smile, and asked me if I'd ever shot a gun. I told him sure, but I didn't go into my story with the bird. I didn't know how he would take it, and I didn't want to risk coming off like a pussy. He asked me what I'd shot, and I told him it was a .22 rifle. He nodded and without pausing said, "That's a great kid's gun. Good for tiny tots and girls. You ever shoot a *real* gun?" So I just shrugged and said no. He asked me if I wanted to. I said sure.

So we stopped at some old abandoned factory. The sun was setting, and everything had this orange glow to it. We got out, and Jeremy opened the trunk. Inside there was this big aluminum briefcase. He opened it up, and I couldn't believe it. There was all this foam padding and there were *six* guns inside! Unbelievable. I was just staring at them, and he started to laugh. I asked him where he got them, and he just said Santa brought them because he was such a good boy last year. "Now these," he said, "are guns." He told me to pick one up. I hesitated, and he told me not to worry, that the safety was on all of them. I asked him which one I should try. He went into this whole speech about each one, and he really got into it. I couldn't believe how much he knew, and I gotta say, I was impressed.

He had a Glock 17, which is like the most used gun right now with cops and very popular on the street. It's got this polymer frame, which is like a high density plastic, which makes it light. It holds 17 rounds in the handle in two stacks. There was a Beretta 92, which is made in Italy and holds 19 rounds. Heavier than the Glock, used by the cops there. Next to that was a Walther P99, which is made by the same guys who made James Bond's gun, which was the PPK. It's smaller, got a really short recoil, holds 19 rounds, and has a super fast muzzle velocity. Then he had some big fuckers. There was a Smith & Wesson .44 Magnum, which is the one used in the Dirty Harry movies. It's more old-school, not a semi-automatic but instead has a rotating cylinder. It is still one of the most powerful handguns in the world, especially with the new .500 model. It weighs a ton and has a huge recoil. Then there was the Desert Eagle .50 – it's as powerful as the Smith & Wesson, but is semi-automatic – it feeds with a handgrip magazine. It's the largest mag fed handgun in the world, and it's made by the Israeli military. The metal has this nice gold colour to it, and Jeremy said it was really popular with the gangstas. They call it a "Dezzy." Pretty cool. And last but not least, there was this huge motherfucker – a Magnum Research 45-70 Hand Cannon. It's about 2 feet long, has a laser sight, and Jeremy said it can shoot a bullet for miles without losing velocity. It was designed for the U.S. army and it can bring down a plane! I couldn't even hold it steady! Actually, Jeremy laughed and said the only one he'd let me shoot now was the Walther, 'cause most of the others would probably break my wrist or dislocate my shoulder if I tried to shoot them. He said when you shoot a magnum it felt like you had just detonated a grenade in your hand.

So, he gave me the Walther. It still felt pretty heavy to me. The metal was all slick, and it had this oily smell to it. He grabbed the Dezzy and we walked into this factory. It was really cold in there, and it smelled like something had died in there not long ago. Really sour, and damp. It was pretty dark. You could only see the windows above us on the far wall, and Jeremy said to just go for a shot at the window. Most of them were already broken, but we saw a couple that weren't. I took aim and squeezed, but nothing happened. He laughed and said he forgot the safety was on, and then he reached over and clicked something on the gun. He told me it was the same as with a rifle really. Just take aim, hold the gun with two hands, let your breath out, don't lock your elbow, and squeeze the trigger gently. So I tried all that, and then there was this ear-splitting BLAM and my wrist felt like someone just hit it with a hammer. I yelled and I dropped the gun. The window was untouched. Jeremy was laughing. He told me I definitely needed to practice. He picked up the gun and inspected it, and told me it was a good thing I didn't scratch it too badly. I asked him what the big deal was. He just looked at me and said, "The big deal would be that I would shoot you here and leave you for the rats." No smile. I waited for him to tell me he was joking, but it didn't happen. He just stared me down. And just when I really started to worry, he laughed and said he was just fucking with me. He put his Dezzy down and came up to me. He told me to try it again. My hand was buzzing like it was full of bees, and my wrist felt like someone stepped on it, but he said to come on. He stood behind me and I raised the gun again, both hands on it. He grabbed my hands, holding them still, and pressed into me. I felt his breath on my neck. His mouth was right by my ear. "Now … aim for the window. Let your breath out. Bend your elbow a little. Gently squeeze the trigger …" BLAM – my arm jolted up like it was yanked on a rope, and the window at the other end of the factory exploded into silver shards, falling to the ground. We both yelled. Cool.

We went shooting a bunch of times. We'd always head out to the industrial area, and I was glad about that. Once or twice Jeremy mentioned going out to the parks out by the highway to try and "hunt" some animals, but I'd say I wasn't into it. He'd say, "Just rats or pigeons, c'mon … it'd be good for you, put some steel in your veins" … or, "You should step it up, just embrace your power, just *be* who you are." He'd look at me with his deep look, like he was mining inside me for something I didn't want to tell him. I could swear he knew about my shooting that bird. He'd hold me in that stare, diving into my brain, and then finally smile and say "Whatever." Sometimes I wonder what would have happened if we'd gone out and I tried to shoot another animal. Maybe none of the rest would have happened. Maybe I just would have shot myself instead.

So anyway, I guess that was the test for admission into the Jeremy Anderson club. For a long time I didn't know if there were any other members – I sure didn't see any. I mean, we never hung out with anybody else. He kept telling me that he could hook me up with his crew, but it didn't happen. I put Agent Smith's voice from *The Matrix* on my iPhone as the ringtone for his calls. So whenever he called, you'd hear "Misss-ter Anderson" in that creepy drawl. It's funny, because even though he had the same name, Jeremy reminded me more of Agent Smith than Neo. Anyways, he finally said one day that he was going to introduce me to his guys. I had to admit I was kind of excited. At first I thought they'd be like gangstas or something, but that wasn't it. These guys were older. Jeremy told me that some of them worked at some investment companies and banks. I never did really find out, but I could tell they were real heavy money people. I couldn't believe it, and I had to admit I was impressed. Jeremy was a made guy. And it made sense to me. Why bother with the kids at school when you could hang out with real players, right? So now I was an official member of the Jeremy Anderson club. It was funny, because I could tell that this wasn't *his* crew. I mean, these guys were all older, and it was like Jeremy was a low-level player for *them*. They were letting him hang with them, but I could tell they were using him. Whatever. He was enjoying himself, so what the fuck, right? I was just glad to be in on the action. These guys were definitely *happening*.

I went to a few wild parties with him. I saw him hook up with lots of girls at parties, and he hooked me up a few times, which was cool, until we got to this party at one of his banker buddies' places – it looked like one of the houses that my mom sold – and I turned around and suddenly I saw him hitting on Tasha. *Tasha!* Can you believe it? At first I couldn't figure out what she was doing there. But then I thought about Tasha's special talents, and I figured it all made sense. She saw me and smiled this 'so good to see you what a nice surprise isn't it past your bed time' smile, like she was so much better than me, or she deserved to be there and I didn't. There was three guys swarming her, all chatting and trying to get a piece. I turned around to get out of there – I didn't want to have anything to do with that bitch, but Jeremy saw me and asked where I was going. I told him I was taking off, but he put his arm around me and steered me back in to the crowd, and I couldn't seem to do anything about it. I tried to forget about Tasha, but there was no way. I lost Jeremy again, and I floated around, trying to get into the scene, and suddenly the bodies parted and there was Jeremy with Tasha on a couch, and he was moving in for the kill. I mean, they were doing more than talking, as in, they were checking out each other's tonsils with their tongues. They came up for air and saw me. Jeremy smiled and waved his hand for me to *come over here and check out this hot bitch!*

The universe was conspiring to fuck me in the ass. Every time I thought something was going to work out for me, I ended up losing. I mean, of all the girls in the world, going to all the parties, *she* walked into *this one*! And she had to hit on Jeremy, or maybe it was the other way around, I didn't care. Now I really wanted to take off, but something stopped me *again*, and I realized that Tasha was going to tell him about me anyway, so, it was like being zapped by the Star Trek tractor beam as I walked up to the happy couple. Jeremy started in on introducing me to her, and she laughed. I told her to fuck off, and Jeremy fixed me with this big 'Whaaat da fuck' kind of look, with her still laughing. I just turned around and left.

I tried putting a little space between me and Jeremy after that. Maybe it lasted a week or two. He told me that she wasn't any big deal. He said she was just another chick, and I shouldn't get so hung up about it. I asked him if he would have hit on her if he knew that we'd gone out, and he said he would. Then he said, "Why do you give a shit? Are you still banging her?" There wasn't much I could say after that. I mean, I was through with Tasha, so y'know, what was the biggie? Jeremy said that chicks were just crazy and emotionally needy, and if I got hung up with that stuff, I'd be finished. He said that men were hunters … that we should never stop moving and taking, 'cause that was who we are. It was in our blood. He said, "Look at Harper. Your brother is getting whatever he wants, whenever he wants it, wherever he finds it." I said, "What about my dad?" He laughed and said, "What about him? I don't see him hanging around here going to parent-teacher night or taking you to ballgames. He's in some other city getting his dick sucked in a hotel room." I should have just slugged him out cold right there, but … in some part of me I felt he was right. I had this tight feeling in my chest, but I sure as fuck wasn't going to let him see how upset I was. He leaned in to me, put his arm around me and said I just needed to get laid again. Couldn't argue with that. Then he told me that if I was still so hung up about Tasha, he'd stop fucking her. Then I told him that he didn't have to do that, and that I didn't care. He cracked up. "This is very funny, man," he said, "but if you keep this shit up, I'm gonna get bored. That would be the worst." I heard him on that. Anything but bored. Bored was the worst. So anyway, I figured this was over, I mean, he said he'd ditch Tasha, and I figured that was that, so, whatever.

A week later, Jeremy picked me up at my place. Usually I just met him outside, and we took off immediately, but this time he started hanging out and talking with my mom. Now, I didn't get why anybody would want to hang around with Lauren for one second more than they had to. I mean, she wasn't as bad as Krystal, but it just didn't make sense. It was like she was trying to be hip, and it was just pathetic. Some of my old pals thought she was pretty cool for a mom, but I just saw right through it. She was always so fucking cheerful, and when my buds were over, she'd all but *run* up to them, saying stuff like "cool" and "right on" and "way" and it just made me cringe. I could tell my buds were laughing at her, but then they said at least she wasn't a dried up old bitch like their moms. I don't know – you should be who you are, and I just think she was trying too hard. Plus, she really took care of her body, she worked out almost every day in the gym with her trainer, so I guess you could say she kind of looked hot for her age. I don't know – it's kind of gross.

So, Jeremy came by, and he just basically walked in after a little knock. I was in the kitchen with Lauren, and he just walked in like he lived here. I got up to go, and he *sat down*! He started talking to Lauren, actually *talking* – I can't remember what they were talking about, but, y'know, Lauren was so excited for anybody to talk to her, and I said, "Hey man, we've gotta go, right?" But he said, "It's cool, we've got time." I was standing there, and at first I thought, 'whatever', and I went to get something else to eat from the fridge. I figured it'd be two minutes and then we'd be gone. Nope. So I went back and started hauling out some turkey leftovers and salad and jars of pickles and rice and potatoes until there was this huge pile on the counter. Both of them finally stopped yapping and turned and stared at me like *I* was the weird one here. Lauren just smiled at me and said, "I didn't know you were staying for lunch," and for a second I actually thought Jeremy was going to say, "Sure." But then he said, "We have to go, but some other time would be great." They were both smiley smiley, and then we finally took off. So we were in his car and I asked, "What was up with that," and he said, "Hey, it's always good to make nice with parents. It pays off later when you want something, or when you get in some serious shit. Besides, I think your mom is kind of hot." I did not want to hear this. I told him that and he just laughed. "Whaddya think, that she's a MILF?" I was now getting angry, and I told him to let me out of the car. He accelerated. He turned and looked at me, and very slowly said, "What do you think I am? Just because I popped your ex, you think I'm going to go for your mom? What do you take me for? We're buds, right?" I mumbled something and let it go. But it was weird, right?

So, a week later Lauren asked me, "Why don't you invite Jeremy over for dinner?" I went all buggy, because I can't remember *ever* having a friend over to our house for dinner. Then I thought, maybe she means to go out to some restaurant, but no, she meant to our *house*. I told her he couldn't, because we were busy that night. She said she hadn't said what night, and I said *'every night'*. That didn't go over too well, and she got all bitchy and pouty, just like a bigger version of Krystal. Sometimes it's hard to tell them apart. Then she said, "It'll be great to have another man here for company," and I'm thinking, 'whaaa?' My dad was away, of course. I didn't know if Lauren was getting any, but I did-not-like-this. Not cool. Nuh-uh. I figured I just wasn't going to tell Jeremy, and I'd keep him away from the house for a while, and hopefully she'd just forget about it or something. But no, she had his cell number, if you can believe that! So she texted him and the next thing you know, dinner was set for Friday. She asked me what she should make, and I told her she should check out the Epic MealTime website. Have you checked this out? It's awesome. It's a couple of guys who make the most sick stuff, all with bacon, fast food, booze and candy. Too much. My favourite is their Fast Food Pizza Cake. They put layers of bacon, meat-lovers pizzas, White Castle cheeseburgers (180 of 'em), extra layers of cheese, more layers of bacon strips, another meat-lovers pizza, about four layers high – it's like 2 feet thick – cover the whole thing in a beer and Jack Daniels batter, and deep-fry it, then put one more layer of pizza, burgers and cheese and bake it again. And then they eat it! I don't think they used all 180 burgers – it looked more like maybe 50, but whatever. These guys are sick!

So anyway, I'm figuring I've just got to suck it up, how bad can it be, right? I'm just happy that Krystal wasn't going to be around. She figured it would be too gross – and for once I agreed with her, so she went off somewhere with her friends. I was surprised that Lauren let her go, but there was a little worm turning in my gut that said that this wasn't a good thing. So Friday night came, and Jeremy showed up, and it looked like he dressed up a bit. I mean, maybe it was my imagination, but I hadn't seen that shirt before, and his shoes were all shiny, and he had these black jeans that were kind of shiny – but then I thought, maybe I was just goofing on the whole thing. So he came in, and Lauren had been cooking all day, and she'd set the dining room table, and I was thinking, 'oh man, we're gonna be here all night, this is not gonna be an eat-and-run. We're here for the long haul'. Lauren was fluttering about the kitchen, opening and closing drawers, checking the oven, clicking the light on and off, lifting lids on pots on the stove, it was like she was on speed or something. She was fidgeting with her hair. It was like she thought she was on a date! This was so fucked up.

So Jeremy came in, and she offered him a *drink*! She looked at me and said, "It's a treat." She had to be kidding. He laughed and said he was actually 19, because he "missed" a year and was redoing his senior year. This didn't quite add up mathematically, but I kept my mouth shut. She offered me one too, and I grabbed a beer. I really felt like getting wrecked, but that wasn't gonna happen here. Later, definitely. So we sat down and Lauren brought in a fucking Thanksgiving dinner, I mean, the food just didn't stop coming. The table was covered in dishes of food, candles burning, all this steam coming off the food – it was like a hundred degrees in there.

So they started chatting away, and it was as if I wasn't even there. Non-stop. I hadn't heard this much conversation in our dining room since … well … ever. Blah blah blah. Jeremy was telling her how delicious this was, and how amazing that tasted, and Lauren was just eating it up. She was blushing. Then Jeremy started talking about how lucky he was to have a pal like me, and how similar we were. He was talking about how his dad got into trouble with the law – I can't believe he was spilling this *now* – and how hard that was for a family, and how he'd had trouble in school in the past, but now that's all over and he understood how important it was to work hard. For a second it almost seemed like his eyes were getting teary. In-fucking-credible! He was a master bullshitter! He said he wanted to be an investment advisor like his dad, but he only wanted to invest in socially conscious companies. Lauren was hypnotized. Then she started to talk about her job, and she mentioned how sometimes she was scared going into some of these huge homes, especially when it's dark, and that she carried a gun with her. Jeremy nodded understandingly. Then, he looked at me, then her, and said his parents gave him a gun for protection as well. The room went silent and I'm thinking – 'we're fucked – we – are – fucked … you are a batshit crazy fucker who has just fucked us …' Lauren looked at him, smiled, and said she understood too.

I thought I was in another universe or something. Jeremy told her that they used to live in a bad neighborhood, and with his Dad not around, and his mom working all the time, they decided to give Jeremy a gun, train him with it, and educate him on "responsible firearms use". Wow. The only time Jeremy saw a bad neighborhood was when we hung out and watched *The Wire*. But Lauren saw the logic in his tale, no questions asked. I could only see the floor, which seemed to be heaving and pulsing with my heart rate.

Then, oh then … wait … check this out, there's more … then he said, "I have it in my car. Would you like to see it?"

What. The. Fuck. This couldn't be happening. Lauren said, "Sure … I'll get mine too," and Jeremy got up and went out. Lauren went to get her purse, and she asked me if I could help clear up the dishes. I couldn't even stand up. I had to be dreaming. This couldn't be happening.

Jeremy came back in with a small, rectangular wooden box under his arm. The box was actually covered in a soft blue cloth, and I could see why. It was beautiful, with all these patterns on it made by small shiny stones or whatever. Lauren called it "mother of pearl inlay" and she was oohing and aahing over it. He opened it up and there was *another* gun that I hadn't seen before, sitting in a bed of purple velvet. He called it a .380 Makarov and it just looked like a small automatic to me. He complimented Lauren on her little .32 snub nose. I couldn't breathe. I staggered away from the table and went outside.

A little while later Jeremy came out and just said, "Let's hit the road." I stared at him. I was speechless. He said, "You really don't get it, do you? Your mom is just dying for attention, and I gave her some. Everything is cooler than cool, because we got a much longer leash now. You should be thanking me. And your dad should be here banging her." That was it. I suddenly took a swing at him, which he dodged easily. He took a quick lunge at me, and I fell to the ground, and he pinned me to the wet grass. He blocked my throat with his arm, and just stared at me. My heart was thudding, and all I heard was the hiss of sprinklers over the slowing whump of my heart. He said, "I told you once not to fuck with me. You gotta grow a pair man. I could fuck you up badly, right now, like I promised I would. But I'm feeling generous because your mom is so hot and pitiful." The heavy dinner was gurgling and boiling in my guts as I gasped for air. "So I won't leave any marks on you. But don't come near me again until you've grown the fuck up. We could be kings together, man, but instead you have to be a hysterical pussy. I got no time for that." And he got up off me, but not before he rabbit-jabbed me one hard into my gut. I doubled-up, all hunched on the wet grass, puking and gasping as he strolled over to his car, which he slowly and calmly drove off into the night.

So it was back to the beginning again for me at school. Or whatever you want to call it. Jeremy totally ignored me, and I didn't give a shit anyway, or at least I didn't think I did. I tried really hard to convince myself that I didn't give a shit, but I knew that I kind of missed hanging out with him. He didn't seem to care. Chicks hung around him like flies on shit. Good comparison that. What my teachers called an apt simile.

So I tried to forget about him, just, y'know, fuck it. As in, adios. Sayo-fuckin'-nara. At school they had elections for the student council, which I always thought was just so much bullshit. I mean, give me a break. 'Oh, I'd like to be president please.' That means I get to do … what? Can I change the school day, or the schedule, or the work, or our rights, or how we're conditioned … uh, I mean, taught? Nope. I can organize a dance. Or a bake sale. Or tell other people to do it. Wow. Oh, and I get to have that on my resumé, so I can get into a better university, or get first dibs on that landscaping job. Ever see this movie called *Election*? It's pretty good. It's about this nerdy do-gooder dweeb in high school who thinks she has a lock on the student council election. But this teacher who hates her guts decides to try and stop her from winning, and he sets up this dumb jock to run against her. All sorts of shit happens. It's pretty funny, because it's basically saying that all this high school culture is really bullshit, just a microcosm for life in general, and people are pretty much fucked up under their appearance of authority. You should check it out.

Anyways, I decided that, like one of the characters in this movie, I was going to run on a platform of total apathy and disregard. So I showed up for the nomination meeting, and basically they told everyone that if you wanted to run, you had to get a minimum of 50 signatures to qualify *after* you make a speech in a school-wide assembly to select the most popular candidates. What a bunch of horseshit. Anyways, I didn't tell anybody what my 'platform' was (didn't have to) and all the teachers thought I was doing so great by getting involved in school politics, what a turn-around, a new leaf, blah blah. So it was my turn, and I walked up to the front of the stage, everybody was there, spotlight on me, and I just started to talk about what bullshit all of this was. I mean, I didn't use *that* word, but I used others like 'hypocrisy' and 'game' and 'systematic propagandizing' and 'exploitive power structures' and such. The place went nuts. Some kids booed, others cheered – lots of shouting, lots of noise. The teachers got real nervous, and I knew they wanted to yank me out of there. I said I was owed my two minutes like everybody else, and there were more cheers. I promised if elected I'd abolish the student government and put an end to these pathetic, hollow promise-making rituals. More cheers and yells. My two minutes were up and I was all yanked off the stage. Democracy in action baby. This is what it looks like!

So I was just going about my bidness, shuffling tru da day, marking time. Taking a little more shit from the teachers, who weren't too happy about me exercising my democratic rights. They said I was being a shit-disturber and a smart-ass (not in those words), I said I was speaking to the truth. Just like Socrates. In my History class, my teacher, Mr. Chatterjee, really thought he could take a strip off me. He went on and on about how I was mocking the whole process of civic empowerment, and I just shrugged. Then all of a sudden, from nowhere, Jeremy raised his hand. Chatty thought he had an ally, and I turned in amazement as Jeremy calmly told him he was full of shit (not in those words) because Socrates and all great political action had arisen from challenging the status quo, and I should be applauded (those *were* his words). Chatty turned red and said they had a difference of opinion, and perhaps Jeremy would like to write a report on it. Jeremy declined the offer. I gotta say, I was pretty amazed that he stuck up for me. As we left class, he came up to me and said, "That took some balls, man. You showed some serious cojones when you went up there in front of everybody and let 'em have it. Very cool." I muttered a thanks, and then he said, "Let's get some beers tonight. And do a little shopping. On me." Without waiting for a reply, he gave me a nod and took off.

Now, like, I didn't know what he had in mind for shopping, but I was always up for some beers.

So he picked me up and we headed out to the mall. Now, I was thinking, why the fuck are we going to the mall? Like, how boring is that? Jeremy wasn't really a mall kind of guy. Me, I could take or leave them. They're good for picking up chicks, though not much else. I mean, if you need to buy something and you know what you want, OK, but hanging around a mall is strictly for kids. I used to go there a lot, but now I'd only go there if I wanted to see a movie, or buy something, or pick up some girls, or hang out with my buds. Or whatever.

So anyway, we hooked up and we were walking through the mall, and I asked him what he needed to buy. He slapped me on the shoulder. "Not 'need', buddy, I'm way past need. Now, '*want*', that's different. And what I want is to buy you a graduation present." I'm looking at him like WTF? Graduation is months away, and what the fuck is he talking about? Does he think my dad won't buy me a present? I started to get pissed off, and he laughed. "No man, no school graduation. Fuck that. I'm talking about 'Graduating to A Set of Balls'. You showed me you've moved into a new class of guy. My class. So I want to get you something to show how solid we now are."

I didn't know what to say. Part of me felt, like, who is this guy to be talking to me like I'm some kid who's growing up for daddy? On the other hand, it did feel kind of good, and getting some new gear was always nice. So we stopped outside this really upscale jewelry place. I looked at him like, 'are you buying me an engagement ring?', and he read my thoughts and said, "A watch, bro. And I got just the one." He held up his arm and there was this smoking watch on it, kind of simple but you could tell it cost serious coin. "It's an Omega Seamaster. It's been the official James Bond watch since *Goldeneye*. Before that he wore a Rolex, even a few Seikos (although those were shit). It's time you got one of these." And like I'm some fucking prince or something, he leads me into the store, gets a clerk, tells him he wants an Omega Seamaster for his friend, slaps down his Visa Platinum card, and that was it. It cost $2000, tax in. "Nice friend you got there," says the salesman. "That's one classy watch." He went to put it in a box and Jeremy said, "No, put it on." So I did. Jeremy held out his hand, we shook, did the fist bump. He laughed and threw his arm around my shoulder. "Now about those beers ...." Buds forever, right? Just like that! It felt good.

So next thing I know, we were sucking back some frosties at some downtown club, real dark, house music pumping some sick beats, awesome light show on the dance floor, real skanky bitches slinging the suds, and we were just hanging, right? Jeremy leaned in close to me and, shouting because it was so fucking loud in there, he told me that it was time he introduced me to some new friends, because they could really help me out. I thought I'd already met his buds at the party, but he told me that he meant some real players. I thought, whatever, sure, that sounded cool. He told me that a pal of his was having a Halloween party at his place. We should go. Now, the last party I went to with him was didn't work out that great, especially the part where I found out he was fucking my ex-girlfriend. I realized now that it was all Tasha's fault, I mean, she must have stalked me or him at that party, or maybe not, anyway, whatever. I figured if she showed up again, I'd be ready to deal with it this time. Jeremy told me that I had to get a costume to get in. I was like, what? I didn't really do costumes, they were for kids or geeks, right? He insisted it was totally part of the fun, and the wilder the costume the better. I told him I had no idea what to do for that, and he said I could just rent one if I couldn't make one, although you got more credit for making one. Whatever. I rented.

So Jeremy took me to this Halloween party at another one of his investment buddies' places, except this time it was at this condo downtown on the 87th floor or whatever. You could see over to Russia from this place. Floor to ceiling glass, corner placement. Stainless steel everywhere, marble, you know? Huge digital panels with changing paintings and photos on them. The whole place looked like something that Lauren would freak over. I know I was. Jeremy was packing a baggie filled with E. He didn't have any costume on. I asked him like, what the fuck? He just laughed. The scene was totally crazy, I mean, there were some pretty wild costumes. They took some serious time to put these together, or at least some wild imaginations. There was one chick dressed like a fuck doll – total beige body stocking, painted on nipples, round red mouth, and she was standing on a little wagon being pulled by some guy. A bunch of Bin Ladens, basically like guys in dusty rags with bullet holes in their heads. There was a giant strap-on dude, a used tampon chick, and then my favourite, a guy dressed up in a tuxedo and top hat, monocle, big cigar, cash sticking out of all his pockets, and all these little human heads attached to his belt. I asked him what he was and he said, "An investment banker." Hilarious. Even better, this guy grabbed one of these shrunken head things and shook out a little pill for me, and you know what that was for, right? Our favourite letter! Mister E! Time to visit with Molly! So I popped it and grabbed a drink and a bottle of water and I cruised around. I watched Jeremy come and go with different people in and out of rooms. At one point I saw him stuff some cash in his pockets. He was doing good business tonight. Then I lost him for a bit, then he reappeared, checking out the ladies. I was playing it mellow, waiting for the glow to hit. He floated over to me and said there was someone he wanted me to meet. I figured it's some babe, and I started to feel real good, so I said 'sure' and he took me down a hall which seemed to go on forever, all mirrored and glowing – I checked myself out and I looked pretty fine – I rented a military general's outfit, had everything – boots, the suit, the belt, the medals – yeah, I looked smart! So Jeremy stopped at this door for a moment, looked back at me with this weird face, kind of serious but kind of winking at the same time, and said "Your life is about to change." I was thinking, this chick is gonna be *awesome*!" And then he opened the door and motioned me in, *and he followed*! Not my idea, but I was feeling warm and beautiful now, so whatever. We went in.

It was another big room (like … how many were there in this place?) with more floor to ceiling windows, and it was pretty dark, which I liked. Just a few big chairs, a sofa, a big motherfucking curved OLED TV, and a little bar which was glowing all different colors, pulsing with the music. There were just a few people in there: two who were necking and looked like they were gonna get funky, and another two or three people sitting around all mellow. There was a few lines laid out on a glass table … I couldn't see much; the only other light than the bar was from the plasma, which looked like it had some old surfer movie from the 60's or something on it. My eyes adjusted a little, although they were probably a little pinned by now, but I saw some huge paintings on the walls. I couldn't tell what was on them at first. They looked like giant mountains or something, but as I stared at them I saw that it was actually naked chicks' bodies from right up close. Cool.

Jeremy steered me towards a big leather sofa chair with this guy sitting opposite. Dressed in a real nice suit, no tie, looked like a stockbroker kicking back after work. Jeremy introduced me – his name was Patrick. This was his place. Jeremy said Patrick could really help me out. I had no idea what he meant, but that was OK, he seemed great anyway. Patrick smiled and I saw his teeth, all totally white and perfect. His handshake was firm, his hands dry and cool. He leaned back and said, "Nice shit Jeremy. Top shelf stuff. Who do we have here? Welcome General! Jeremy told me you're a real good friend of his. Said you're gonna go places." I told him he had a real cool place, and I loved his costume. Man was I high. He smiled again. "You want a place like this? You want a costume like mine?" I said sure. He said, "Did Jeremy tell you anything about me?" I told him not really. He said he's on the Board of Directors at like, five different Fortune 500 companies, he's the Chairman of a couple of different charitable organizations, one that works with NGO's in Africa battling malaria and AIDS, and another that distributes free laptops to really poor kids all over the world. Wow. He told me that he did all this stuff without leaving the couch he's sitting on right now, and gets blowjobs while he's doing it. Now I was really impressed! He asked me if I thought there was anything wrong with being a huge corporate stakeholder, being philanthropic and getting blown all at the same time. I tried to think about this, but basically I couldn't see any real conflict here. He said he was glad to hear that, because that's the way the world worked. He asked me if I could see myself in his position. For a second I wasn't sure what he meant. Was he asking me to help him out? Was he asking me if I was trying to compare myself to him? He smiled, but not like he was playing with me, more like a laid-back, easy-going smile that was just so confident and relaxed. He looked at Jeremy, then at me. He said, "You can get it all, but how bad do you want it, because you've got to want it bad to go all the way to get it." I wasn't sure exactly what he meant, but it seemed so right and beautiful that I just nodded and went 'yeah'. "So how bad do you want it?" I just stared at him like maybe this was a trick question. "What would you do to get it?" I started to laugh. It just seemed funny. Patrick smiled even more, laughing a little. His laugh sounded like waves on a beach ... then I thought maybe it was the surfer movie, but I turned to look at it and now there was some nature movie and there was all these shots of glaciers and ice … very cool. I stared at it because it was so fucking beautiful, all shiny and blue and clean. I heard my name and I turned. There's Patrick. He said, "Do you know how many people steal every day and don't get caught? Do you know how many people kill every day and don't get caught?" I shook my head. He said, "Do you know how many people get away with breaking the rules, every day, every minute, and never get caught? Most people actually. The smarter you are, the more rules you can break, until you realize that the rules don't even really apply to you anymore. In fact, there really *aren't* any rules. We just pretend there are. Listen to me … This is the way the system works … .We're on a big rocket ride to infinity … to the stars. But rockets are really all about the tip, the top, and that's where the real players are. The rest, they're in the fuel can, which is 99 per cent of the rocket. That part burns up on the trip … it falls back to earth … it exists only to propel the top part into space. But there's only so much room at the top … you have to fight to get in there. You have to stake your ground. You ever hear of Nietzsche?" I stared at him and laughed, because I knew *exactly* who Nietzsche was, and what Patrick was saying, and it was all so perfect, I could tell that this moment was totally fucking significant and heavy, but also beautiful, like great things were going to happen for me now. Patrick leaned in towards me, I could see his eyes had these two little points of light, little pictures of icebergs shining at me, he reached out and cupped his hand behind my head, pulling me in real close to him. I could smell his cologne. He smelled like dark, old wood, like spices. He said, "You want to be big, you gotta do big things to stand out. Be smart, be tough, be beautiful. Rise above all the little people and you can have whatever you want." I felt his hand squeeze my neck a little, and it was like he'd communicated some very heavy message to me, like I could feel it going straight from his hand to my neck to my brain.

"Do something incredible," he says. "Rise above them all."

After that, I floated around the place, and it was all so warm and beautiful. I knew after that night I'd have to do something … something incredible. Now I knew what Jeremy knew. But I never figured on killing those kids. That wasn't part of the plan. Blowing the school up into atoms – *that* was the plan. But I still wasn't quite there yet.

Anyway, after that I was kind of a changed man, y'know? I mean, it was like this guy Patrick, who obviously had it all happening in his life, had kind of just laid it out for me, and somehow … I don't know … I just really got it. I mean, when I think about it now, it wasn't all that different from my dad or Harper. They're pretty much the same as this guy really. It's just … like, I guess maybe because this guy wasn't my family or something. It just really sank in. You know, without all the family bullshit or whatever, like sometimes you just listened better to a stranger. Whatever.

So the next week or so I was walking around school like I was in the clouds. I felt like a superman, like Nietzsche's *Ubermensch*. I did all my work, I was totally *there* in class, I walked around like a fucking struttin' player, y'know?

And then Jeremy got busted. Or almost busted. They found some weed and some pills in his knapsack. Of course, here's where it got interesting. Jeremy didn't usually carry a knapsack. Those are for losers, or geeks. You need a book, you carry it in from your car. Done. The knapsack wasn't found in his locker. Again, who uses a locker? Juniors I suppose. But he was seen with the knapsack earlier, and when the school security patrol fell on him, it was *near* him. Not *on* him. He was in the student lounge, and he got a heads-up on the bust just before they ran in for him. They said he ditched the knapsack over a few couches. So anyway, he's got a history of dealing (that's why he got bounced from the other school, right?), and a few eyewitnesses who said they saw him with it. Now that surprised me. Why rat out your supplier? Maybe someone else wanted his action? Whatever. Anyway, they tried to squeeze him, but he didn't crack. His mom was called. I got a quick look at her and the step-dad. A couple of glittering wraiths with hard, tanned, chiseled faces. They glided into the principal's office, barely looking up from their phones. They were in there for hours (I heard it was dark by the time they left). I heard the mom was some some big facial reconstruction surgeon, and she had hooked up with this guy who was a power lawyer, and he laid it on thick. Seems it wasn't such a slam-dunk case for the school. He promised them a royal ass-fucking if they wanted to go to the mats on this. Jeremy was back in the halls the next day. Like it was business as usual (which it wasn't, at least for a while). The admin promised him the same surveillance trip they pulled on me. They told him his days were numbered if he "kept up with his behaviour." Since he was an adult now, he could face criminal charges that would stick. He didn't seem fazed by any of this. Actually, I saw him smiling. Fuck, that guy was cool.

But you know, it kinda spooked me, but not in the way you think. I mean, Jeremy was a smart guy – like I said, he didn't seem to have much trouble with the schoolwork, same as me. Sure, he did a little extra-curricular business, so, whatever. It all just seemed to get to me. I looked at the work I was doing, and, I don't know, I just got tired of it. I just felt like … what a good little robot, y'know? I didn't see the payoff in it, right? Here's my gold star! What a good little boy! Now shut up and move along. It wasn't enough, and it just felt like a game, and I'd already decided I was going to be bigger than that, and do things on my own terms, like Patrick said. Why play this stupid game? Follow all the rules just to … what, get fucked over in the end? We saw this documentary in class about how Halliburton and all these oil and gas companies started drilling for natural gas in farmland in the U.S. They offer what seems like decent leases to all these hicks and hayseeds, who naturally go for it. Then they drill, and they do this thing called "fracking." which is basically pumping all these chemicals and water way down into the ground to loosen up the oil and gas. Problem is, all these people get their well-water totally polluted, their animals get sick, they get sick. They even show these people holding lighters beside their water taps, and the water *catches on fire* from gas that's seeping through. How fucked up is that? And the corporations get away with it. There's hundreds of thousands of these rigs all over the United States. Fuuucked up! Now, who do you want to be? Mr. Hayseed who's getting fucked over, or Dick Cheney, who's sitting on his yacht, which he flew to on his jet, eating oysters and drinking champagne and getting blown by a high-class hooker? Hmmmm … let me think about that for a second …. You know, I'd like to be a world-saving saint, some tree-hugging, sign-waving soldier for justice, but there's no payoff in it. The game is rigged, and since we've all got to play, I'll be a winner, fuck you very much. I didn't make the rules, right? I'm just moving around the board like everybody else. And Jeremy, he was walking around like a bear on a tight chain. Nobody went near him, and that started to piss him off. Even the water parted when he jumped into the pool.

So, I got tired of being Mr. Superman the nice goody-goody. Lousy dividends, as Harper would say. And then it hit me. Like the start of your favourite concert, when one second you were all talking and waiting and the sound was all mushy with music and people talking and shouting, a million different conversations and ideas floating around, and then WHAM – the light dies and everybody's energy goes straight to the stage in a roar of total, focused attention and expectation, and the light and sound kick in for that first moment and you are *there* in a way that just pushes out every other thought or feeling – you are locked in to this moment and understanding – it's like the truest thing you could possibly know, right?

Well, my epiphany came at a football practice. What could I do to make my mark? Make my statement? Rise above them all? Be better and bigger and show the world I was not to be fucked with … that I was a king of men? What could I do to the system that had fucked me over and that had robbed me of who I could really be? I knew it had to be something big, and something that, if I did it right, couldn't be pinned on me even as I walked around knowing I had done it, and letting the gods know I had done it and couldn't be touched? I didn't want to hurt anyone, but I wanted to smash my way through to power and status and have people say under their breath, "That is one serious motherfucker." They'd see me then. Like Jeremy. Nothing could touch him. And then I knew. I knew, as sure as I knew anything, that all this shit had to go.

Into atoms.

Into nothingness.

And I was the guy who was gonna make that happen.

Sometimes I still can't believe it myself. Anyway, like I keep saying, I'm no psycho or anything – I wasn't planning to hurt anybody, not even the janitor, y'know? No, I had it figured that the school would blow over the Christmas break, so everybody would have an *awesome* Christmas light display as the place went burning and flying into the sky. *MERRRRRY CHRISTMASSSSS!!!!* You know, I figured this would really put me over the top. Now, I'm not stupid or anything – I knew I had to keep it secret, but then I thought I could let it *become known* but only in ways that couldn't lead them to really pin it on me. I could develop the rep for it, but not the proof of it. It would drive the cops crazy, but I'd get major respect from Patrick and Jeremy. I'd be moving in a whole new class, up where the view is always beautiful and the air is clean and thin. On top of the mountain, the penthouse condo! Where the class of people who *make things happen* get to party. Where the Supermen live. Like the Joker said, "You wanna make an omelette, you gotta break a few eggs." I'd learned that these people exist, and I wanted to be one. Simple as that. And I was going to make it happen.

So … you're probably wondering what my plan was. How I put it all together, right? It wasn't that hard really. You have to be smart, which I am, and know your chemistry, which I do. You've got to do your research. So how do you make a bomb? Actually, it's pretty easy. Anyone can make a little boom boom, but I was looking to make something major league. You need some serious chemistry smarts, and more than a little cash to pull this off. Neither of which was a problem for me. I even made part of the bomb at school in the lab – I told my teacher it was for the Rocket Club. Of course, that only worked for the early stages of the initial detonation charge. When I moved to the secondary charge, the big blast, well, that had to be done at the space Jeremy rented. But I'm getting ahead of myself again.

At first I was thinking about nitroglycerin, because it explodes so intensely, but it's way too unstable to transport or manufacture. Any little bump can set it off, and even making it can cause it to explode. You can freeze and desensitize it until later, but that can have the opposite effect, and it can then fail to detonate, or you can add ethanol and stabilize it, but again, it can go dead on you. Nitro is really an old-school explosive – way too unstable to work with now. There's this movie *Sorcerer*, where these guys who are total losers are working in this shithole mining camp in the jungle. They're offered a ton of money to ship containers of nitro across the jungle in these old trucks. It's their ticket out of that place where they're kind of trapped. I like that idea – taking a big risk to change your life, and the bigger the better. So anyway, for my masterpiece, I went for a combination of RDX and PETN for the main charge, and nitromethane liquid for the initial detonation. RDX was developed during World War II by the British as an explosive more powerful than dynamite. They wanted something that would really take care of the German U-boats, whose hulls were pretty thick. They called it "Research Department Explosive" or RDX. It's pretty easy to make – you combine nitric acid with hexamine, and then freeze it until it crystallizes. It's about fifty percent more powerful than TNT. If you mix RDX with PETN, you get this great plastic explosive called Semtex. Way more powerful than TNT. But it's hard to get this baby going – that makes it stable to work with, but it needs a lot of energy to detonate. So that's why I used nitromethane liquid for an initial charge. This stuff is a liquid explosive – looks just like water. You just mix nitromethane and Windex and you get a juice that's twenty-five percent more powerful than TNT. You can store it in any kind of container, and you just need a standard blasting cap to set it off. So, together with the main Semtex pack, you've got a motherfucker of a bomb. Pretty sweet.

It's pretty cool watching stuff explode, right? I mean, it's not like I'm a pyro or anything, it's just the way it is for guys. You take a room with ten guys, I guarantee seven of them have been into fire or exploding stuff at some point. I can't explain why, really. It just feels … so … free and fun and … I don't know, exciting. Girls have dolls, guys burn shit. It's a laugh. Why do you think they do it so much in movies? There's a lot of excellent movie explosions, right? I think some of the best are the *Die Hard* series. In the first *Die Hard*, you've got an FBI chopper exploding mid-air, and of course the top of the building exploding as Willis jumps off with a fire hose. Awesome. *Die Hard 2* has that great bit at the end when the bad guys are getting away on the plane, and Willis lights the leaking fuel trail with his lighter and it catches up to the plane – KABOOM! Another great series would be the Terminators. When Cyberdyne blows up in *Terminator 2*, that's pretty great, and in *Terminator 3: Rise of the Machines* you've got an excellent "end of the world"-type deal when Skynet launches the nuclear attack, and everybody else does the same, wiping out most of the planet. That's pretty great. *Mission Impossible* has that helicopter exploding in the tunnel – the flames and rotor blades just miss Tom Cruise – TOO BAD! *Swordfish* has that awesome opening scene where this chick wearing a vest packed with C4 and ball-bearings runs out into the street, and she explodes, sending a massive shock-wave with these ball-bearings tearing the shit out of everything. You circle around the blast like in the *Matrix* – it's pretty fucking cool. *Transformers* had the Qatar Air Force base wiped out by Blackout's blue-flame pulse weapon – how great would it be to have that? *Transformers 2* had, I think, like 114,386 explosions – how do you top that? *Pearl Harbor* has the *USS Arizona* being bombed to bits. You see it from the bomb's view – cool. *Fight Club* (one of my fave movies) has all these office towers blowing up at the end with The Pixies' "Where Is My Mind" wailing on the soundtrack. I mean, that's it for me! That movie is just *it*, you know? The whole Project Mayhem, I can really get with that. All the hypocrisy and bullshit, all the lies, fuck it, just tear the playhouse down. I think it's really about just trying to make a statement, trying to be heard, and I could relate. He goes schizophrenic, totally creating this alter-ego to wreak havoc on society. Then the guy has serious second thoughts, but it's too late. You gotta accept who you are. Man up.

I told you already I used nitromethane liquid, some blasting caps, some large plastic containers, and Semtex packages for the main charge. Now, the research for this was something that I did pretty carefully, or at least I thought I did. Later, when I told Jeremy, he told me I was a fucking idiot for having done it on *my* computer. He told me the cops were able to trace my searches, especially since they weren't re-routed. He told me I should have done it from a series of different internet cafés, and use some different accounts. He was right, I should have thought of that. But those places are such a drag to hang in. And I just didn't think about my computer – it's like a part of me. That wasn't my only mistake. But anyway, you get your information all together, and then you start purchasing. I also forgot that credit card purchases can be traced, and I used them a lot. Whatever. You can find tons of different supply houses all over the country, and it's good to purchase small amounts at different ones, *which I did*, so that was smart. Harder to trace or find a pattern when they're scattered, right? Once you get your supplies, you need a place to work. Your home is a really bad idea, unless you live alone, with no neighbours. So, you need a space. Storage rental units are good, but you have to go in really off-hours. You also need a supply of water, so you have to bring that, because they don't have any. You've got to build up the lab slowly, so you don't attract attention. The RV idea in *Breaking Bad* was pretty smart actually. Anyways, it took about three weeks for me to get it together, which I thought was pretty good, because I could have done it in two days. Anyway, I had basically six or seven weeks to get it together before the Christmas break. Time enough, but not a lot of it. I had to really focus, but I figured if I just disappeared completely, it would attract attention, so it was tough. I wasn't going to tell Jeremy. I just wanted to own this all by myself, y'know? I mean, I liked him – he was basically my only pal now, and I knew he was kind of in a bad place, even though he'd never say it. But I just wanted this thing to be mine. Then I thought, maybe I'd let him in at the end … maybe. But things didn't work out that way. As I got deeper into the project, I obviously wasn't hanging out with Jeremy that much. I turned him down on a couple of shooting dates, and backed out of a party, and then that was it. He cornered me and wanted to know what was going on. Like, what was wrong with me? I really thought about it, and he just totally squeezed in on me and I couldn't think of any way to dodge him that he would believe.

So I told him. He was stunned – absolutely silent for, like, forever. He just stared at me, drilling holes into me with those icy blue eyes of his. And then it happened. His mouth turned up at the corners, and this big, glowing grin just spread across his face. He threw his arms around me and whispered, "You are the *man*, brother." He was squeezing the air out of me, shaking me like a rag doll, and laughing, with great big whoops and hollers. He stood back and checked me out, like he'd never seen me before, and said "*Damn*" and "*Too cool*" and stuff like that. He wanted to know all about it, and at first I was real shy about it, but he kept pressing, and then said he had a space we could use, which would be great for testing it too, and he knew guys in demolition, so we could get some stuff for making it, and he started getting a total hard-on for the whole thing, and before I knew it, I had a partner. Actually, not a partner. He told me that I was the boss, and he was just there to learn from *me*! That made me feel pretty fucking good, right? He told me this over and over again. I was the master, and he was the disciple. This, from Jeremy! Far-fucking out!

One night he came around to pick me up, and he tossed me a memory stick that he wanted me to check out. It had this old TV series from the 70's called *Kung Fu* on it. I figured, cool. Lots of awesome chop-sockey, right? He told me about how it was a Bruce Lee project, but the Hollywood studios stole it from him because they didn't think America was ready for an Asian hero. Anyway, he says it's really full of cool philosophy, and he said it reminded him of us. I didn't know what he was talking about. So we watched some, and it *was* pretty cool. It's set in the 1800's. The main character, Kwai-Chang Caine, is a half-breed (half Chinese, half-American) raised in this orphanage by Shaolin monks and taught philosophy and mad Kung-Fu skills. He kills the Emperor – big mistake – and is forced to run! He goes to the United States and wanders around, having all these adventures. The guy who plays him is icy cool and every episode has a great fight. Anyway, there's lots of great scenes of him being trained by all these super-cool monks who school him in being philosophical and learning Kung Fu. Real heavy master and disciple stuff. Jeremy said I was like the Shaolin masters, and he was the young disciple. He told me I knew more than I thought, but I wasn't so sure about that, because he was the one who was always quoting from it. What the hell did I know about philosophy, really? Whenever I got hung up about something, Jeremy said, "*When you cease to understand, then you will know without understanding.*" Which is what Master Po, one of Caine's teachers, told him. I really like this, because basically I realized that it's bad to think too much. I could really get behind that. Just go with your gut, y'know? When Jeremy was helping me set up, I was telling him about all the stuff we needed to do, and he said, "*It is wise to prepare.*" Just like that. That's what Master Po said before Caine had to walk across a pool of acid on this little wood beam. Sounds kind of obvious, but it's true. I told Jeremy that I was worried before about telling him, and that we had to keep this totally secret. If anybody else knew, we'd be fucked. He totally agreed. He said, "*Men do not beat drums before hunting tigers.*" Right on. Sometimes I'd get really overwhelmed by what we were doing. I mean, like, it was huge, right? I'm not saying I was really scared or anything, but still, it did kind of get to me sometimes and make me, you know, kind of worried or whatever. Jeremy, never. He was like a bullet, on the way to the target. Total commitment. He'd see me get freaked a little sometimes, and he'd remind me about the first episode of Kung Fu. Caine meets Master Po, who is blind. Caine says, "*Of all things, to live in darkness must be the worst.*" Po just smiles and says, "*Fear is the only darkness.*" It became our motto. It's pretty amazing once you realize that if you get rid of the fear, you can do pretty much anything. The only thing holding you back is yourself, really. I realized that this is what Patrick was talking about. All those guys who've made it. That's the secret to getting the key to the shiny condo. Just step over the line, take that deep breath, you know. It's just a matter of will. That's what Patrick was telling me. Greatness comes from, you know, getting over your fear of whatever is holding you back. It's so simple. I felt like laughing. Whenever I sensed the worm starting to turn in my gut, I just pictured great things, like Patrick in that condo, up in the clouds, looking down on the city like a god. Jeremy never wavered. Whenever I'd get the jitters, he'd just grab me by the shoulders and say, "*Fear is the only darkness.*"

Now it was *Ubermensch* time. So we got into it. We started moving stuff up to this old farm about an hour out of the city. There was nothing around there. The place was used to be some kind of industrial farming facility. A couple of big buildings, like old hangars, with nothing but a few steel tables and what looked like old pens for keeping pigs or something. Place kind of stank, but mostly it was just a big, damp space. There was no water, but Jeremy said we could bring some in. He got these big tanks delivered with like fifty gallons in them. No electricity either, but he got us a generator. Then we were in business. He asked me how long it would take to get a test bomb made. I told him I had no idea, and he just laughed. He said he appreciated a no-bullshit, honest response.

It took about a month. Longer than I had thought, but then again, I figured if the test went well, then we were pretty much done. It only left us with a few weeks before the Christmas break, but it would be enough time. It would be a great Christmas – the best any kid could wish for. '*Hey everybody, look, the school's gone! Must have been that old boiler!*'

Jeremy said that we should do a test like in *Black Sunday*. I had no idea what he was talking about. He told me it was this movie where there's this wacked-out Vietnam vet who flies the Goodyear TV blimp over the NFL football games, and he decides to build this awesome bomb filled with ball-bearings, sort of like in *Swordfish*, and he's going to fly into the Super Bowl and set it off. Crazy. Jeremy told me there's this scene where he tests a tiny version of the bomb first. He's working in an old barn, sort of like ours, and this farmer stumbles in and asks him what he's doing. He gets the farmer to stand right in front of it – he tells him it's a new kind of camera. *He* goes outside, and BANG. The whole barn wall is perforated with these holes, and, well, no more farmer. Jeremy was laughing as he told me this, and I got the feeling he thought we should try it out ourselves. I told him that wasn't the idea. He shrugged and said, "Whatever."

So, we were sweating it out in that fucking freezing farm, putting this thing together. It went pretty smoothly actually. We did a test, and we didn't kill anybody. We drove about three hours out of town. We took a 4x4 so we could really go off road. Jeremy had scouted this area, and he found some construction site for a subdivision that had just started. We found one of those giant holes that they dig for foundations, but this one had deeper holes for concrete pillars or something. Anyway, I don't know how deep it was. We used raw fuse cord for this one (you know, the old-school lit fuse you see on cartoons) because we just wanted to see if the charge worked. We knew we'd be going with a timer eventually, but, whatever. Anyway, this fuse cord is supposed to burn through anything. We set out about 50 yards of it, jumped in the car and took off. We're driving real calm on the utility road, and then BLAM – there's this fucking mushroom cloud behind us that almost shook the car off the road. Holy fuck! We had to grip the dashboard just to control ourselves from not speeding the fuck out of there.

At first we couldn't believe it. It worked. This was real. We figured we were in complete control at this point. We never thought there might be seismic monitors at that construction site. Shit.

So anyway, we had the bomb pretty well figured out. We needed to do more work on the fuses. This was a little more complicated, because we needed a timer. Remember – it was my idea to blow the *school* to bits, not the people in it, right? So, we did some research online about timer fuses. Pretty complicated actually. There's lots of different detonators you can get, pressure activated, temperature activated, and timed ones for sure, but we were dealing with a time period of *days*, so it had to be a really good one. You can get extended timers, they're called 555 fuses or something, I can't remember, but it's a circuit that emits a delay beep every minute, so it sets the time back by a certain amount, not as much as the amount that is passing … it's a complicated circuit, but you can get up to 80 days on one. We only needed a few days, but there was no way we could do another test – too much boom-boom, too much attention, and besides it was almost time for the Christmas break, so we had to go for it. I was worried about the beeping. Even with the place empty, a janitor making rounds could hear it. I knew I'd have to open the timer up and find the chip for the sound and remove it, and hope it didn't fuck up the whole circuit. Either that or build some container to muffle the sound.

We'd put it all together, so now all we had to do was plant it. We argued over where the best place for it was. So many great choices, y'know? There was the cafeteria, for all the shit they passed off as food. Or the Math office, for all the grief they caused us. We talked about the boiler room, I mean, kind of appropriate, right? But Jeremy thought that would be a bad idea because the janitors might spend a little extra time in there before taking off for the holiday, and it might get found. The gymnasium was no good – not enough atmospheric compression for the initial blast, although it felt good to think about all those change room lockers melting, and those fucking stinky showers. So we figured it had to be a classroom. The Science lab was the final choice, because it also had some combustible gas lines, and it also had some pretty wild chemicals in there. Could make for a nice light show. Maybe get a nice fiery fetal pig flying across the firmament!

So Jeremy and I watched the days creep by as Christmas break got closer. Good old Christmas. When I was younger, it was kind of a big deal I guess. We'd get some great presents, and sometimes when Luke was around, he'd really try and treat us all like we were royalty or something. Once, he took us all to Paris! Now that's what I call Christmas! But, you know, he hadn't been around much lately, and now I got stuff pretty much whenever I wanted, so I didn't see Christmas as such a big deal. I figured it was pretty much for kids and losers. Or religious nutbars. I knew Jeremy felt the same way, but he kept going on about how great it was. What a bullshitter. If this guy stepped into a church he'd burst into flames. And like I said, whenever I asked him about his family, he just said, "boring" and that was it. Now he was telling me that he really loved Christmas? I figured he was just fucking with me.

It was the last day before Christmas break, and there was a big assembly. You know, the Drama club had some lame skits, and the choir was screeching Christmas carols, and the Multi-Cultural club did speeches about Hanukah and, what was it … Kwanzai or Banzai or whatever. Everybody had to get in on the act. What a brain freeze. But it was a great time to sneak in to the Science lab and plant the goods. We were snaking down hallways like escaped convicts, y'know? Had to watch out for the hall monitors. We got to the hall with the Science lab, but there was a fucking hall monitor right there! He was camped out, leafing through pamphlets on sexually transmitted diseases pinned up on the bulletin board. Freak! We couldn't get past him, so Jeremy decided to set up a diversion so I could get in. He decided to go downstairs and up the stairway at the other end of the hall, over by this guy. It was risky, because he had another hallway to get down, but it was the only way. He disappeared. I waited. Felt like forever but it only took two minutes before he appeared at the other end, walking towards the guy. The dude saw him and immediately set out in his direction, doing his tough-guy thing. Jeremy started talking about feeling sick, and wanting to go home, but I didn't hear the rest as I made my way to the door to the lab. We'd stuffed the lock jamb with tinfoil before, so even when the door was locked, it could be opened because only the knob was locked. I opened it silently and slipped in. I took the package out of my knapsack, and then the timer. I connected them, set the timer to a 12 volt battery and put it in a cabinet below the gas valves. Two minutes later I was done. I looked out, and Jeremy and the guard were gone. The dude was probably walking him to the office. Sweet.

I'd set the timer for Christmas Eve. I figured that was perfect. Just when everybody was partying, and watching *The Grinch Who Stole Christmas* – KA-BLAM! Take that, Cindy Loo-Hoo! *"But Santy Claus, why are you blowing up the schoolhouse? The Grinch rubbed his whiskers and thought for a second …. Because, dear child, you'll be free of its bullshit, at least for a while!"* Man, this was going to be the best Christmas ever! I could hardly sleep for three days before Christmas Eve. Even with all the partying that me and Jeremy were doing – it was like I was permanently awake! Everybody noticed that I was super-hyper. Lauren and Krystal looked at me like I was buggy, and I guess I was. Luke was back in town, and he figured it was because I was so excited to have him back – which is true in a way. He'd brought me back some uber-cool swag, and I managed to pry most of it out of him before Christmas day. He got me this Think Geek Electric Guitar T-Shirt – too cool. It's got a guitar on the front, and a series of magnetic circuits sewn in to it. You get this magnetic pick, and when you turn on any Bluetooth device, you can *play the shirt*! Or it comes with this little amp you can put on your belt. You just put your fingers on the fret lines, and strum with the pick, and you get these awesome guitar sounds! How cool is that! I also got this turntable, the iON Profile, which transfers vinyl records directly onto my iPhone or iPod. I got Luke some stainless steel ice cubes. You just throw them in the freezer, and they don't water down your expensive scotch. I got Harper these mini-knife cuff links. A tiny folding knife in a ¾ inch cufflink. I got Krystal a Yo-Yo mouse. It's this wireless mouse that recharges by using it as a Yo-Yo. It exercises your wrist, which can get messed up from sitting at a computer for too long. But the coolest thing of all was the Body Vibe dumbbells that I got Lauren and Luke. These are rechargeable vibrating dumbbells. What happens is that the vibrations in your hands cause the muscles in your hands and arms to quickly contract and relax, which burns more energy in less time. So, you get more results for less work. I'm not even going to tell you what those cost.

Finally, school broke for the holiday, and it was a couple days before Christmas, and me and Jeremy were hanging out, and he went out to his car and came back with a wrapped box which he gave to me. I looked at it and felt kind of shitty because I didn't get *him* anything. I mean, c'mon, was I *supposed* to give him a Christmas present? He said, "Merry Christmas" and that he "thought I'd really like it," and I mumbled, like, 'uh, I got you something too' and he laughed because he knew I was full of shit. He said, "Your present to me is the light show we're gonna see on Christmas Eve." I mumbled some more and he said, "Open it up now if you want." So I figured, OK, and it was the Think Geek Electric Drum Machine shirt, which was kind of like the Electric Guitar shirt, except, well, you know. You touch different pads and get all these totally cool drum sounds. You can even program it to play repeating patterns. Then I figured, OK, cool, I'll give him the Electric Guitar shirt! It'd be perfect. And you know what? It was. I went and got my shirt, re-taped the wrapping paper, and when I gave it to him he was blown away. "You see?" he said, "It's like we're brothers or something! How cool is that?" My new brother. We jammed right there, laughing our asses off and laying down all these heavy metal techno licks. That was probably the most fun we ever had, right there. I wish I could have stopped the clock on my life right then. That was a perfect moment for us, just … well … I try to just remember how great that was, but it doesn't work. It burns a hole inside me just thinking about that. After that, it pretty much all went to shit.

So we were hanging out and it was two days before Christmas Eve. We were totally hyped and nothing we did was going to calm us down. We went drinking, we checked out some games at my place (he still hung around too much, talking to Lauren, but whatever), we went to a party, but nothing was good enough. Finally it was Christmas Eve and we were at this party. Well, we started out at my place, and Lauren wanted us to stay, but I didn't want any of that. Jeremy was like, "Well, we could stay for a while." I looked at him like, 'oh man, you must be kidding – not tonight for fuck sakes!' We got up to go and on the way out, Lauren wishes him a good Christmas and happy New Year and she *gives him a kiss*! I mean, it's just a little one, but what the fuck? He smiled and seemed to hug her just a bit too long. We left. I didn't say anything.

We figured the best place to watch the fireworks was from the mini-mall, which was about two blocks from the school. There was this shitty little bar there. We'd always go and get drinks because they were too stupid to check my fake ID, and we'd just sit and drink beer and eat fries and shoot the shit. It would probably be pretty quiet on Christmas Eve too. So we went there and they told us they are closing at 9! Fucking Christmas! So we hung out there and had a couple of beers, and then decided to cruise the neighborhood until show time. We could get away with that. After all, there was no law against driving. Driving drunk, sure, but we made sure we only had a couple, and we were well below the limit on Jeremy's portable breathalyzer. So, we drove around, pumping tunes, not saying much. The tension was pretty heavy. I kept eyeing the clock. We cruised, not saying much. I lit a joint and Jeremy tossed it out the window. He said we don't want to take any chances with cops on the road tonight. Right. I was getting more and more amped. I stared out the window, just looking at all the stupid Christmas lights, all of them passing by in a blur, all the houses, everything the same. All the cars, all the mailboxes, all the nice trees, and I thought, I've got to get out of here. Not just the car, I mean, like, this place, right now! This fucking vacuum-packed nowhere. My ticket out is about twenty-seven minutes away now. We're driving. The headlights flashing against snowy trees. I close my eyes. It was all a milky white blur, turning, moving slowly, rolling along. Turning, gliding, Jeremy was trying to get us into the best position for the main event, a few blocks away, just a few turns from the school so we could turn and see it while it was still in full detonation. The car was hot, and I was sweating, so I opened the window. The cold air felt good on my face. We moved more slowly now. Fourteen minutes to go. We rolled to a stop at an intersection. I stared at the lights. It was taking centuries for them to change. Red. Red. Red. Red. Red.

Yellow. Yellow. Yellow. Fuck! C'mon! Yellow. Yellow. Yellow. Fuck! Green. We went. Slowly. Controlled. Jeremy drove totally calm. Like your granny. Eight minutes. He turns down the tunes. He turned to me. "We want to hear it all." I told him he wouldn't have a problem with that. It was going to be mighty fucking loud. As in, the universe-exploding loud. I looked at Jeremy. His face was a mask. No emotion. His eyes were shining from the headlights. He stared straight ahead. His mouth was a thin, straight slit cutting across his face. I was jumpy as all fuck, I kept shifting in my seat, jittery and turning my head this way and that, biting my nails, rubbing my hands on my jeans, clenching and unclenching my fists, running my hands through my hair. Jeremy was like a driving robot. A skin-covered statue. I heard the tires slowly crunching through the snow as the car came to a stop. He cut the engine.

Two minutes.

One minute.

Thirty seconds.

And …

Zero.

And nothing happened.

We couldn't fucking believe it. We sat in the car for like, half an hour. We drove right up to the school, just staring at it, as if staring at it long enough would make it happen. Forgetting that the blast would take us too. But nothing happened. Nada. Nobody home. We stared at each other, and Jeremy got this look in his eyes that I didn't like. That cold stare, where his eyes got all small and there was just one little pin of light in them. Two hard, polished stones reflecting a little picture of me in each of them. I could see his jaw muscles twitching. We said nothing. We drove around forever. Silence. He dropped me off at home, and finally he spoke. "We're going in there." I just nodded and got out.

Now, like, I started thinking that, well, maybe this wasn't *supposed* to happen, y'know? Maybe I was getting a last chance to pull out of this thing. I thought about this, and then I thought that I'd never been into this mystical stuff. I'd never thought that there was some god who was playing with his cosmic X-box and laughing at me. And if there was, then fuck him because I didn't like this game anyway. So, I got my head straight – something went wrong, and that was it, and it was fixable. I already knew that Jeremy would probably kill me if I told him I wanted to back out. But then I thought, I'd already shown that I could do it, right? I mean, I made the thing, and did everything except actually blow up the school – wasn't that good enough? It was like having the best part without the worst part. I told Jeremy this and he said it was bullshit. Who would believe me? He said he could tell people his dad helped fake the moon landing – didn't really make people believe it. Talk was cheap. Actions spoke louder than words. In this case, like, deafening. I heard that, but still, I didn't know. Then he told me that we couldn't just leave it there. It's not like it wouldn't go unnoticed. And our prints were all over it. I told him we could go in there and get rid of it. He told me I was half right. We were going to go in there, commando-style, to check it out and re-set it. I figured he was nuts. There were cameras everywhere, and motion detectors, and the place was locked up tight. He'd got it figured out though. "The place is locked up, except they get deliveries of supplies and stuff, and that's when the alarms are turned off. We go in then. We'll be masked, so the cameras won't see our faces." He was a fucking evil genius. And to prove his point, he reached into the backseat and pulled out a bag with two Halloween masks. One was the Joker, the other was the *V for Vendetta* mask, which was also kind of a Joker riff if you ask me. He asked me which one I wanted. I went for the Joker. I started to think I was living in *Fight Club*. That was totally like us. I'm Ed Norton, and Jeremy was Brad Pitt-Tyler Durden. We were best buds, we both realized the system was full of shit, we'd planted a huge bomb – it was all the same. Even the chick, Marla – that's Tasha. But then I was also thinking, if I was really Ed Norton, then, that meant I'm also Tyler Durden, and that meant I was kind of, like, nuts. Which didn't make me too happy. But it did feel like I was losing my mind. But then, how would I know if I was losing it? Like, if I was crazy, then wouldn't all this just seem normal to me? But I was also *thinking* about this, so I couldn't be crazy. But Ed Norton was thinking about it, and he *was* crazy, wasn't he? That also means that I'm Jeremy, and I'm pretty sure that isn't right. And what about Ed Norton, I mean, how am I supposed to feel about him? He does try to stop Operation Mayhem, even though he started it. *He was sorry!* Same as me. Did that make it OK? He got the girl in the end, with Marla standing there, cradling his gunshot face, holding his hand as the buildings fell. Not me. I guess that's the movies, right?

It was Christmas Day and everybody all over the world was opening their presents. I mean, all good Christian capitalists were. Lauren and Luke staggered downstairs at about ten. Luke got in late last night, and he looked pretty bleary. Harper wasn't here yet, but he was on a flight and was expected in a few hours. Krystal still hadn't got up, and everybody was surprised to see me up and dressed. Wasn't hard, seeing as how I didn't sleep at all last night. My brain was like my smartphone, buzzing away furiously, lost in some drawer, with Jeremy on the other end. I knew we were going to break into the school again, and it was eating me up. We all opened our presents. Nice. Luke was trying to be super-cheerful, talking about going skating, or tobogganing, or skiing, or hiking, and we were all looking at him like "easy Mr. Winter Enthusiast", or "take a Valium" or whatever. I mean, we were glad to see him I guess, but he was really putting on the Dad thing a bit thick. I don't know, it just seemed weird. I knew we all missed him, and it was good to have him back, but he sounded like a sports announcer, all hyper and *super-daddy*. Lauren asked me what Jeremy was doing today, and I looked at her like, "what kind of stupid question is that?" I was sure he was doing his own moronic family thing like we were. Whatever. She said if he wanted, he was welcome to come over and spend some time with us. She was sure Luke would like to meet him. I told her to forget it. I had about ten messages from Jeremy. Not like him. My stomach was knotted-up into a tight ball of flame. Luke and Lauren got into major breakfast mode, cooking up waffles and eggs and sausages and home fries. I had no appetite, but I choked down a bit. I told them I had to go out and see Jeremy, and they both insisted he come here. I had no choice. I couldn't get out today. I called Jeremy and he said OK, he'd come by later on. I slummed about the house, played some *Call of Duty: Black Ops*, and watched the clock.

About two o'clock he showed up, carrying a big bunch of flowers that he gave to Lauren, and a present for Krystal – a gift card to some chick clothing store. They're both going ga-ga over him, and Luke gave him this little smile. "Pretty classy friend you got there," he said to me. Yeah. Whatever. I paced around like a tiger in a cage, waiting to take off, and now Jeremy was all Mr. Cool and Charming. He was chatting up my dad now, who just ate it up. Something about fixed liquidity and dividend yields. Whatever. About twenty blocks from here we've got a bomb that just *won't* go off, and Jeremy was just chatting away like he hadn't got a care in the world. I didn't get it. How did he do it? Finally, finally, *fucking* finally he said me and him had to take off to exchange presents with some other pals, but he'd have me back in a couple hours for Christmas dinner. Everybody stared at him like, "Isn't he so charming and mature and wonderful" and I just wanted to laugh. Oh man, was he good at this bullshit! We drove for five blocks before he pulled over. He told me that there was a shipment of school supplies coming in two days. That's when we were going in. I asked him how he knew that, and he told me that he brought the caretaker a bottle of Scotch as a "last-minute present" – and he asked him if he could get in to get some work. The guy said no, but the delivery came up in conversation. Then I asked him what happened if it went off before then, and he looked at me weirdly. "Well then, Watson, I guess we'll have the case solved, won't we? Are you retarded or something? Look, Sundance, if it goes off, then I suggest we head to Bolivia – they got some great banks there!" He laughed coldly. Now I looked at him like *he was* the retarded one. What the fuck was he saying? Was he *high*? Who's Sundance? And what the fuck did he mean by that Bolivia bank stuff? I knew he was playing me, and I wasn't in the mood to be played. We went to the mall but it was closed, so we ended up in a Starbucks where we drank coffee for two hours. I was totally wired. He dropped me back at home. "Merry Fucking Christmas," he said as I leapt from the car. Yeah, and fuck you too!

I went back inside my house, and there he was, the Mighty Harper had returned! Standing there in the kitchen, looking over the inside of the fridge like he'd never seen one before, taking his sweet time over just taking out a beer, there was my big brother. He turned and saw me, the fridge still open, his face lit by its chilly blue light, he flashed his million-dollar grin as he cracked a beer open. The fridge door closed quietly with its eight thousand-dollar sigh. I walked over to him, but what I really wanted to do was run into his arms and tell him I'd fucked up, and that he had to save me. But I didn't. I just walked over to him. He handed me the beer. I took a swig. Handed it back. He smiled.

"What's going on, little man?" I shrugged. "Merry merry." He took a long pull on the beer. "That's what they say. So how's your year?"

I shrugged again. Said nothing.

"You makin' a splash?"

I asked him what he meant by that, and now he shrugged. "Are you standing out from the crowd?"

I told him I was playing it all cool, and that I just wanted to get out of there. He smiled, took another pull on that beer, and started singing something about "knowing when to play them, and when to lay them." I had no idea what he was on about. Was there something about this day that made people even more fucked up than usual? I asked him how long he was staying.

"You get me for four days. Best I can do. I got a big New Year's thing in Bali. Very sweet." I wanted to ask him if he'd take me with him, but I knew what the answer would be. He saw something pass over my face, I don't know, I just stared at him for a second, maybe a second longer than I should have, but I swore he could read my mind.

"It's not as bad as you think it is, brother. This too shall pass." He waved his hands over me like he was making some kind of spell or something, and then started laughing. "Lighten the fuck up – that's an order! It's fucking Christmas, for fuck's sake." He gave me a rough hug and I had to hold my breath to stop myself from melting in his arms and blubbering like a little girl. Save me. Yeah, right. Not.

Anyway, I guess if you haven't figured it out by now, I really hate Christmas. It's just such bullshit. Even without buying all the presents, which I *can* get behind actually (because who doesn't mind getting some good swag) there's this whole idea of suddenly everybody's going to get together and be lovely and have fun with their dysfunctional family. Probably the greatest hypocrisy in the Western world, and the biggest con-job ever. Just thinking about it gets me back in the blow-up-my-school mood, really. So anyways, it was Christmas dinner time, and blah blah fucking blah. Luke and Harper were basically having a business meeting, Krystal and Lauren were like two generations of Barbie dolls bending over for their men, and I sat there trying hard not to throw up, or throw the carving knife at somebody's head. It finally ended. Joy to the world. Luke said we should watch a great Christmas movie, and everybody groaned, because they knew that meant it was time for him to basically show off his home theatre. He put on some old dusty flick, *Miracle on 34th Street* I think it was called. Something about Santa Claus and some kid – I can't remember, it was so fucking slow and dumb; watching it felt like getting stoned without the feeling-good part. I must have fallen asleep fifteen times. If you want to watch a good Christmas movie, I've got a few. I recommend *Santa's Slay*, which has Santa as the son of Satan (ever actually think about those names?) who actually lost a bet with his dad and had to be a good guy for a thousand years. But now time has run out, and he's in a different mood, like, a *killing* one. I can identify. *Bad Santa* is one of my faves. Billy Bob Thornton as a thief posing as Santa who's gonna rip off a mall with the help of his midget elf accomplice. I love it when he gets shot in his Santa costume on the front lawn of some kid's house. Nice image. *The Ref* was pretty good too. It's got Dennis Leary as this thief who gets stuck at this snobby couple's house on Christmas and he takes them hostage. They are total pricks. They hate each other, and their kid hates them. They drive Leary crazy. It's great until it wimps out in the end. Actually, it's pretty much my family, except for the happy ending.

Anyways, a couple of days later, Jeremy and I sat parked in front of the school, watching the delivery guys wheeling in stacks of paper and whatever. Jeremy started to pull away. I asked him if he'd changed his mind. He gave me another one of those looks that I had really learned to hate. He said, "No, Watson, but we don't want my car parked outside just in case it gets picked up on the cameras, or some nosy neighbour remembers it." I had to hand it to him, he thought of *almost* everything. We drove a few blocks. He asked me if I had my mask. I nodded. He handed me this big black overcoat, kind of like Neo in *The Matrix*. It hung long and covered everything. He told me, "We'll be on camera most of the time – we don't want to give them any recognizable clues." We got out. "Keep your head down as we get to the school. Don't put the mask on until we get to the door. Put it on with your head down." Yes, dad.

We snuck in the supply door at the side when there was nobody there. We were inside and slinking down the halls in double-time, stopping at every corner. I started to head up the stairs to the science room and Jeremy grabbed me, shaking his head. What the fuck was he up to? He motioned down the hall and I looked at him like 'Whaaa?' He pointed to the caretaker's office. I had no idea what he was on about. He half dragged me there and motioned for me to stay. He darted in the open door and I saw him go to the key collection on the wall. Of course – the science room would be locked now. He grabbed the key. It was Mission Fucking Impossible time. My heart was pounding so hard I could swear that Jeremy heard it. We were like two rats running down the halls. I heard the voices of the delivery people down the hall, around the corner. We were up the staircase, darting to the science room. We were in. He stood guard while I checked out the package. It was there just like I left it. I stared at it. Jeremy was looking out the door down the hall. I had no idea what to do. Everything looked right. I was sweating like a pig. No, I was sweating like a sweating pig. My eyes were stinging, my heart was jackhammering, my hands were shaking. I took a deep breath. I had to do something. I was afraid I was going to blow us up right there if I fucked with this thing. Then I saw that one of the leads had come off. It must have come loose when we pushed it to the back of the shelf. Shit. Jeremy made a "ssst" sound and I looked up. Was someone coming? He pointed to his watch. I nodded, did what I had to. I got up. He motioned me over. He leaned right into my ear. "We leave slowly and carefully. No running dashes. Keep cool." I nodded. Yes dad.

We headed down the stairs. The delivery guys were leaving. How would we get out when they went? The door was right by the caretaker's office. He'd hear us, or see us if he was hanging out there. Then, we got a gift. He took a broom and headed up the opposite staircase. We were totally in the clear. Out.

Now, I know you're probably thinking, how did I set that little fucker this time? I mean, I didn't tell you what Jeremy and I figured out, right? We still had a lot of Christmas break to go, but he wanted to see the place go sky high, and I could get behind that, right? So, we decided on New Year's Eve. Actually, this was even better, right? *Happy New Year!* And then, KA-BLAM. What could be better, really? This would be the ultimate, right? That's what I kept telling myself anyway. Right. So, it was a few more days before New Year's, and Jeremy was hanging around my house *a lot.* I mean, I even came home a couple of times when I was out doing some stuff and he was *there.* I mean, he didn't call me or anything, he was just hanging out with Luke and Harper, playing Wii or Xbox, or just … *sitting around!* Now, how weird is that? Who did he think he was? Was he trying to take my place or something? Maybe I was Ed Norton. All I heard from Lauren was "What a great young man he is" … even my nuclear bitch sister told me she thought he was "cute" and "cool." My mind was losing cabin pressure.

I had this dream where I come home from school and Jeremy is sitting in my kitchen having dinner with everybody, but it's like from the way they're talking he's not Jeremy … it's like he's *me.* He's telling them about school today, and they're laughing and talking and chewing away, all happy family. I walk in – nobody even *sees me.* I mean, I'm standing there, and they're all just eating away, passing the mashed potatoes and the peas, and having a wonderful time, and I'm standing there shouting at them, and nobody even looks up. Then I go and pick up a plate of food to throw it at Jeremy and my hand goes right through the plate. I'm a fucking ghost! I try to pick up a knife, nothing happens. Then he looks up, and he sees me. I mean, he really sees me. He smiles. I scream.

So, what's that about, right? Maybe I should just start hanging out at his place? How would he feel if I just started pretending to be him, living at his house? He's looking at me so smug and all, like he's got it all figured out. Whatever you say, Holmes!

It was New Year's Eve, and we were at this bitching party back at Patrick's condo. I can't even remember much of what happened that night. Actually, that's bullshit. I tried to forget it all, but even though I was totally fucked up, I remember most of it. I was putting everything I could find into my mouth. Drinking, smoking, did a little E, the usual. Jeremy pretty much left me on my own for most of the evening before midnight – he was totally wired. He kept disappearing behind different doors with different girls, downing drinks almost as fast as me, snorting rails endlessly, and I could see he was moving a lot of product. I just felt like I was in a different world from everybody else. I mean, I should have been right there with him, right? This was my … no, *our* big moment, right? I don't remember even hitting midnight. But I remember the next morning, hurting *real* bad, waking up on the floor in the grey dawn.

Jeremy stood over me. Stared straight down at me.

He wasn't smiling.

He said, "I'm gonna kill you."

So, you know, like, right. He leaned down, and I was just lying there, with my head exploding, and my throat is swollen shut and feels like it's made of sandpaper, and my eyeballs feel like two pissholes in the snow. He looks brand-new. His mannequin-model face, with those two little sparks in his eyes.

"Nothing happened. Again."

I didn't know what to say. Which is what I said. He pulled me up and said we got to go back in. I told him there was no way I was going back in there before school started up again. He stared at me and I could see those muscles working in his jaw. I really thought he was going to lose it. Finally he took this big breath and said, fine, but if it got found before we could get to it, he was going to be really fucking mad. Really? Like, what was he now? I told him whatever, and then I didn't see him for the next week before school started.

So, we went back, and it was the same old routine, except for the bomb that was stuck in the back of a cupboard in the science room. Now, I was pretty flipped out, of course. But my real worry was Jeremy. The guy totally avoided me, which I didn't actually mind, but it was freaking me out a bit. I was waiting for a chance to get in to that science room to get *rid* of the fucking thing. I mean, I guess you figured out by now that I defused that fucker the second time, right? It was like I got a second chance when it didn't go off at Christmas, and I figured why fuck up twice, right? Me and Ed Norton. So, when we went back in I totally disarmed that bitch. I disconnected the main leads from the charge, so nothing would happen. But I still had to get rid of the thing, right? You don't just leave a bomb sitting around, right? But I couldn't figure out why Jeremy was being so cool about it all.

Until the second semester assembly. Happened right after we got back.

Which I always skip because it's boring and useless.

Which all students are supposed to attend.

Which was when the bomb went off.

This *wasn't* supposed to happen. I'm telling you, I had totally changed my mind, and I'd made it so it wouldn't happen. It's like a total blur, really – I still can't believe it. It's like I have to see the YouTube news clips to believe it really happened. I watched all these clips of fire, and people crying, talking about hearing a big explosion. There were some videos shot inside too. It ripped out a big chunk of the top floor, and some of the lower level as well. You couldn't see any bodies, but everything was just … gone. Black smoke, twisted metal and grey ash everywhere. Most of those videos are gone now. They pulled them on account of the families. Everybody's phones ringing all the time. Tons of cops and fire trucks for days. All sorts of TV and media trucks were all over the neighborhood, strangers were knocking on everybody's door looking for interviews. A fight broke out at the supermarket – seems some camera crew wouldn't leave when they were asked to. Somebody lost it when these news guys stuck a microphone in their face. "*Tell us how you feel.*" The TV had nothing else on – it was on every station. Same with the radio. The mayor called an emergency meeting of parents at the rec center. They were going to bus everybody to a few different schools in the area. It would take a week or two to figure out. They offered all these shrinks and doctors to come in and talk to everybody. I hadn't heard from Jeremy at all, which I kind of figured would happen. So much noise, so much attention. The air was thick with it. Everything was a constant throb of muted sobs and hollow looks from everybody.

I knew I should feel pretty fucking terrible, really. And I did.

I guess that's what happens when 18 kids die on a Tuesday morning at school.

Lots more were really hurt bad. Burns. They said there might be more fatalities.

I didn't know what to do. At first, I figured it was best to just appear totally flipped out like everybody else, but it was really hard. I mean, I felt bad because everybody was just totally fucked up about this, but *I* wasn't. At least, I didn't think so. At first. I mean, I felt bad in my head, but it didn't seem to translate to my heart. Then I got fucked up about that. I mean, all those kids were gone, and their families would be damaged forever, I mean, like, you don't just get *over* that, right? I knew this would be bad. That's why I didn't want it to happen – not with kids dying. But then the more I thought about it, the worse I started to feel. Not sad, but … *heavy*. Every part of my body weighed a thousand pounds. Even my guts. I would wake up, and my heart would just start *pounding* like I'd run a marathon. I couldn't get out of bed, and I was exhausted. I didn't even want to eat. It got so that I couldn't even breathe – I felt my blood racing, and I couldn't even catch my breath. I just wanted to get fucked up and forget about it, but that *wasn't gonna happen*. They don't make drugs strong enough for that. Too bad. You know, they say that when you do really bad shit, you get an urge to confess about it, like it will make you feel better. Like Raskolnikov. I don't think so. No matter how fucked up I felt, I thought that coming clean on this would just fuck more people up, and that would fuck me up more, and then it would just be another clusterfuck of fucked-up-ness. I didn't think I'd like that. Of course, you may be wondering what I'm doing right now, but wait. The story's not over. When it is, you'll see that that choice was made for me, so, whatever.

So, like I was saying, Jeremy totally avoided me. I figured that was OK, but after a week or so I figured it would be OK to hook up. I mean, we always hung out before, and if anything, it would look weird *not* to hang out a bit now, right? And I'm wondering, I mean, he was so into this thing, why brush me off now? When am I gonna get to step up with his crew? But I guess I knew deep inside myself that this wasn't going to happen. I didn't want to admit it, but in some dark place inside me, I knew I'd been shut out.

We both got moved to this other school in the neighbourhood, and one day after class I stopped him on the way out. He pretended like I didn't exist; he just stepped past me. Something in me snapped, and I shouted out his name in the hallway. A few heads turned. So did he. He walked back up to me, and I saw him put on his nice guy mask. But he leaned in to me and said, really quiet, "We don't hang now. Done deal." And he started to walk away. I stood there, stunned, like what the fuck, right? I caught up to him and I said something about that being bullshit, and he turned and I didn't even see his hand come up – all I know is all of a sudden I was up against a locker. He was in my face. "Really, bro," he said, "you've seen me mad. This is best for both of us. Time to saddle up and go our separate ways. Best for both of us. OK?" Now, I should have just listened to him, but there was just one little thing that was bugging my ass, right? Like, how did that bomb go off? Now, I don't know about you guys, maybe your bombs go off by accident, but mine don't. That means, well, you know what that means, right? And I needed to hear him say it.

But he didn't. At least, not then. I told him we needed to talk. He said no. I said yes. It was like we were having this fucking lovers' argument or something – what an asshole! I told him I wouldn't stop until he agreed. He stared at me and I could tell he was trying to decide whether to just do it or get rid of me or whatever, but he finally said OK. He told me he'd come over to my place on the weekend. Just like old times.

So it was Saturday morning, around 11 or something. I got up and I heard voices downstairs, and before I even walked into the kitchen, I knew he was there. Lauren was there with him, in her *bathrobe*, and they were making breakfast! I guess Krystal was still in bed, whatever. At first they didn't even seem to see me – it was like my dream again. Then Lauren turned around, and she seemed a little embarrassed.

"Hi honey, how are you holding up? Jeremy was just helping me with some breakfast." We all sat down like we were in Denny's or something and we tucked in to a pancake breakfast, with sausages, eggs, coffee, everything. Lauren was yakking away, going on with Jeremy, asking him about his Christmas, about anything except what's happened, and I was staring at her like, "Hello … don't you know that 18 kids are dead?" Only after he shrugged and said nothing did she get all serious, and she started in on "the accident." She couldn't believe such a terrible thing would happen, so tragic, those poor kids, yadda yadda. Then Jeremy said, "The police are still investigating – they say there was a bomb y'know." I stared at him, my fork in mid-air, pancake chunks hovering. What-the-fuck-was-he-doing? He looked at her, then me, then back at her. Lauren leaned in to him, as if she needed to hear better. Her robe slipped open a little, revealing a bit too much of her fake tits. "Oh my god, I heard that, but I can't believe it," she said, with terrible, intense disbelief. She hadn't moved back in her seat. Jeremy kept going. "Yup – the fire department found traces of some kind of explosive, and they said the blast didn't look like it could be a boiler explosion anyway. It was upstairs in the science room, so that couldn't be the boiler." I put my fork down. I looked at him, and cleared my throat before I choked.

"How about we take off? Breakfast was great, mom, but we really need to go." They both looked at me like they just noticed me *again*. Fuck, this was annoying.

"Hey man, your mom cooked all this food, let's just finish up and then we'll leave, OK?" Lauren smiled and patted his cheek.

"You're so sweet, but it's OK, you boys can go." Jeremy said we should at least help with the washing up – *un-be-fucking-lievable* – and he got up and started clearing plates. Lauren got up with him and they went to the sink. I could swear he leaned in to her a bit too much as he placed dishes in the sink, but I figured I was just being paranoid.

We took off. Jeremy was driving so fucking slowly, like, *at* the speed limit. It felt like we were going in slow motion. We exchanged glances.

He said, "No sense in getting pulled over now, is there? We're on a list already, right?"

I bolted upright – "What the fuck are you talking about?"

"The list of students involved from the school, right?"

"What do you mean, *involved*?"

"I mean, just, you know, being moved and all. Survivors, whatever. We just don't want to raise any more radar blips, right?"

I shrugged. Everything always made sense with him, after he finished playing with my mind. I didn't have to ask him where we were going – I knew it was up to the barn where we put it together. I didn't think this was a good idea, and I told him so. I mean, like, we made a bomb up there.

"Yeah, I know what you're thinking," he told me, "but it's like hiding in plain sight. They never think of looking in the most obvious places." I wondered how he knew this, and how this place would be "obvious" anyway, but I didn't say anything. Actually, we didn't say much for the rest of the ride. It took a lifetime to get there. I didn't know why we were going all the way out there to talk, but I figured what the fuck. I didn't want to set him off, so I figured I'd let him do this his way.

We pulled up to the farm. Everything looked the same. We sat in the car a minute. He looked the place over. We finally got out and headed into the big barn. It looked the same as when we left it, I thought. There were still a few bits of gear there, which was funny because I thought we had cleaned it out completely. Jeremy just stared at me, and I stared at him. Like two cows. Finally he said, "We're done. We had our big show. I don't know about you, but I feel a whole lot better." I fidgeted with a voltmeter that wasn't supposed to be there. I told him that I felt pretty shitty about it actually. He made this big-daddy-exasperated sigh. "Now, that's what I was worried about. I was worried about you the second time. I had to go back and check. I saw the leads taken off the timer. Naughty-naughty. You wimped out. I had to make it right. See, now I know that you can't really man-up to this thing, and now that it's *done*, well, I got more worries than I want."

"You think I'd rat on us?" I blurted out.

"It's crossed my mind, Watson, and I obviously can't afford to have you pussy out on me. Maybe you want to go away and be somebody's bitch for the rest of your life, me, I got other plans."

Now I got pissed. "You think I would do that? You think I'm retarded?"

He stepped towards me. "I don't know actually. Very worrying, man. I mean, I know you're not retarded, but you can be a bit of a pussy. You do lack some *cojones*, right?"

I had no idea what he was talking about, and I was getting angry and confused. "First of all, I don't get with this Watson thing. I'm not your sidekick. Second, I *made* that fucking bomb, not you. *You* were Watson, not me! And I don't know what cojones are."

He laughed that condescending laugh. "Cojones are balls, man. What you need more of. As for the Watson thing, whatever. It's just because I love you."

"*Fuck off!*" I yelled. If there was one thing I knew, it was that he had no fucking idea what that word meant.

"Now, c'mon, is that any way to talk to your best bud? I could be your brother, you know. I'm practically a member of your family."

I figured he was trying to piss me off, but I didn't know why. He was walking around, walking nearer to me, and even though his voice was friendly, chatty, I was getting scared.

"Look man, it was a great ride, but I can't trust you. You're acting all jittery and scared, and that shit attracts attention. I'm going to make it easy for you."

I didn't know what the fuck that meant either.

"Yeah, I know you're confused, and that's part of the problem. Not quite enough balls, not quite enough brains. Aren't you curious why there's some gear here? Didn't we take it all away?"

I nodded.

"Aren't you wondering why I've been hanging out so much at your place?"

I told him I didn't know what he was talking about.

"C'mon chump, are you blind, or just dumb? I've been there more than you over Christmas. What do you think I've been doing there?"

I told him I don't know.

"Yes you do."

"No I don't."

"You're lying to yourself, and to me."

I couldn't breathe. He was just a few feet away from me now.

"You know, Lauren is a great woman. Really special. You have no idea. She really deserves more attention than jet-setting Luke gives her. Which is why she puts out so much, right?"

"FUCK YOU," I yelled. I wanted to find more words to hurl at him, but I couldn't think of any.

"Oh man, c'mon. Who are you? Own it baby! You know she puts out, and why shouldn't she? She's fantastic man. I *know*."

And right there I realized it. My heart was pounding so fucking hard, I swear he could see it. He saw me sweating, I knew that.

"Don't look so surprised man. You told me yourself that both Luke and Lauren were getting some on their own. So?"

I found the breath to garble out the words. "You are seriously fucked up! I'm outta here."

He laughed. "Man, like I don't think you're the best judge of mental health. Seeing as how you're a mass murderer and all. And, uh, you gonna go out to the road and hitch? See how well that works for you. Take a breath boyo, and let me finish explaining to you how this is all gonna end."

He sat down, almost next to me. He was talking, but I couldn't hear. I was *trying* to hear him, but my heart was beating so hard I could feel my blood filling my ears. I was underwater. Except I felt like I was on fire. I was dizzy, trying to suck in big gasps of air.

"See," he says, "this is what I'm talking about. I tell you I've been banging Lauren, who's a total MILF, and you're ready to pass out. Now, how are you gonna hold out if the cops start questioning you."

"Why should they do that?" I whispered.

"Oh boyo, you don't have the best record at that school, right? Just ordinary questioning, and I'm thinking you're gonna fall like a house of cards."

I looked at the ground. My eyes filled with tears. I hated myself for that, but I couldn't help it.

"It's OK," he said. "You're gonna cop to this, and that will be that. You'll be famous, in your way. It's what you wanted, right?"

I'm shook my head.

"Oh man, stop lying to yourself. Stop it."

"What about you?"

He put his arm around me. "Nah. It's just gonna be you, buddy."

I stared at him then, hard. He looked so relaxed, so at peace.

"No, it's just gonna be you. They're on their way here now. Anonymous tip. They'll find you, and even if you run, they'll find this gear. With your prints on it. That'll just be the start of it, but you'll go along. And that will be that."

"What about your prints?" I was panting now, and the floor was heaving below me. Then I see he had gloves on. I didn't. Who wears gloves? Then I realized he's planned all this.

"They'll find a few receipts stashed back at your place. This and that. Oh, and Lauren will swear that I *was* hanging around, but a lot when you *weren't* around, and besides, she's kind of sweet on me now, so, like, I'll be there to comfort her. Tasha might even say something about how you'd talked about doing it. So sad. But … there's nothing to tie *me* to your craziness. You're done. Own it, brother."

He checked his watch. "Look man, I'd love to hang around, but you're about to get busted, so …" He started to leave, turning away from me. That was *his* big mistake. Well, fuck, who knows, like, where he made his mistakes, but this was one of them for sure. See, he didn't figure just how worried I was about *him*. No, he just figured I was so freaked out that I was totally out of control. But, I'd already had a feeling I might be in big trouble. Which is why I brought my Glock. Yeah, he didn't figure I would have my shit together enough to be packing. That was my Christmas present to *myself*. I pulled it out from my coat pocket. My hand was shaking. I swear he could hear it, because he turned back around to face me when I leveled it at him. I had to give him credit, he was pretty cool about it.

"What – oh man! Are you joking? That's great! *Now* you're growing some stones? What, you're gonna shoot me? How smart is that? You want the cops to show up with me shot here? What's one more, right? C'mon, man …"

I had both hands on the gun, it was shaking like crazy. I told him to just stand there, because there was no way I was going down for this alone. No way, no how.

"What," he says, "you gonna *shoot* me, really? Looking into my eyes, you're gonna do that? Hell, even I can't do that. No man, that's cold-blooded shit, that's not you. And you aren't gonna shoot me in the back either, because that's cowardly shit, and I can see now that you're no coward. Forget it man.

Just put it down and breathe." And with that, he turned around and kept walking.

Now, I don't know about the rules of shooting dudes, and what counts for guts or cowardice, but I *told* him to stay, and he *saw* my gun. But I couldn't look at him and squeeze that trigger. Couldn't do it.

Which is why I closed my eyes.

And fired.

About five or six times.

I opened my eyes, and he was lying there, blood already seeping out of him onto the floor, falling down between the wood floorboards into the straw below us. Just like that little bird. I stood over him. His eyes looked different now. Dull. Grey.

I'd like to tell you I felt horrible, like, 'oh my god what have I done' kind of thing, but … no, no bullshit now. I mean, I didn't feel *good* about it – I'm not a psychopath, no matter what they'll tell you. I just … didn't feel anything really. And I know, some people will say that makes me a psycho … but, I don't know … I just felt … tired.

I sat down next to him, his blood pooling around me. I didn't know how long I sat there. It felt like a while. I figured he was bullshitting me about the cops. Or maybe he did but they were too busy getting coffee. I didn't know. I took his keys and got into the BMW and started to drive. I don't remember driving home.

So, here we are. Can you see all those red and blue lights? Lighting up the room like my own little rave. Seems like every cop in the country out there. I guess Jeremy wasn't lying after all. I don't have too much more to say right now. I don't know what's gonna happen to me. Somehow I don't care. I know I should, and maybe later on I will. That sounds kind of stupid.

I know it'll be bad. Actually, I'm glad. Really. I'm just so … fucking tired. All I want is to close my eyes. I just want to go to sleep. Wake up as somebody, anybody, else. I'll never get past this. I can't see how. I can't see anything really. The drain has burped the last of me. But don't worry, I'm not gonna do anything *stupid.* That would be a lousy end to this movie I think. I hate those endings – too much of a downer. But I will take off this dumb mask, I figure I owe you that much, and besides, *everybody's* gonna see my face by tomorrow. So here goes. Hope you like what you see.

CREDITS

Nick Lowe, "I Love the Sound of Breaking Glass," *Jesus of Cool*, Radar Records, 1978

Gottfried Benn, "One Night," *Sämtliche Gedichte* (Stuttgart: Klett-Cotta, 1998), p. 299

John Darnielle & Peter Hughes, "Love Love Love," *The Mountain Goats - The Sunset Tree*, 4AD Records, 2005

ACKNOWLEDGEMENTS

To the following readers who gave their thoughtful reflections on the early drafts of this book: Erin Agnew, Laurie-Shawn Borzovoy, Daniel Brooks, Mark Brownell, Peter Dick, Brenda Nietupski, Noel Palmer, Sky Pape, Lori Roth, and Lincoln Stewart;

To Koom Kankesan for great insight and advice on the story and all things writerly;

To Luciano Iacobelli and all the Quattro Staff for their belief and support;

And most importantly, to my wife Debbie Hiscock for all the support and ideas and wise feedback all the way through the writing of this book, without which it just … simply … wouldn't be,

My deepest gratitude.

In memory of my dear friend, Philip Kates.

Other Quattro Fiction

Traitors' Gate by Nicholas Pengelley
Dempsey's Lodge by Eric Wright
Inheritance by Kirsten Gundlack
Oatcakes and Courage by Joyce Grant-Smith
Terminal Grill by Rosemary Aubert
World of Glass by Jocelyne Dubois
The Sandbar by Jean-Paul Daoust
Texas by Claudio Gaudio
Abundance of the Infinite by Christopher Canniff
The Proxy Bride by Terri Favro
Tea with the Tiger by Nathan Unsworth
A Certain Grace by Binnie Brennan
Life Without by Ken Klonsky
Romancing the Buzzard by Leah Murray
The Lebanese Dishwasher by Sonia Saikaley
Against God by Patrick Senécal
The Ballad of Martin B. by Michael Mirolla
Mahler's Lament by Deborah Kirshner
Surrender by Peter Learn
Constance, Across by Richard Cumyn
In the Mind's Eye by Barbara Ponomareff
The Panic Button by Koom Kankesan
Shrinking Violets by Heidi Greco
Grace by Vanessa Smith
Break Me by Tom Reynolds
Retina Green by Reinhard Filter
Gaze by Keith Cadieux
Tobacco Wars by Paul Seesequasis
The Sea by Amela Marin
Real Gone by Jim Christy
A Gardener on the Moon by Carole Giangrande
Good Evening, Central Laundromat by Jason Heroux
Of All the Ways To Die by Brenda Niskala
The Cousin by John Calabro
Harbour View by Binnie Brennan
The Extraordinary Event of Pia H. by Nicola Vulpe
A Pleasant Vertigo by Egidio Coccimiglio
Wit in Love by Sky Gilbert
The Adventures of Micah Mushmelon by Michael Wex
Room Tone by Zoë Garnett